THE PICTURE BOOK

THE PICTURE BOOK

Susannah Keating

William Morrow
An Imprint of HarperCollins*Publishers*

HarperCollins books may be purchased for educational, business, or sales promotional use. For information please write: Special Markets Department, HarperCollins Publishers Inc., 10 East 53rd Street, New York, NY 10022.

FIRST EDITION

Designed by Nancy Singer Olaguera

Printed on acid-free paper

Library of Congress Cataloging-in-Publication Data has been applied for.

ISBN 0-688-17888-X

00   01   02   03   04   RRD   10   9   8   7   6   5   4   3   2   1

To Sam, Maggie, Lily, and S.,
my love and eternal gratitude
∞

Acknowledgments
∞

The author would like to thank Lydia Vagts for her enormous expertise. Sarah and Giulio Codacci-Pisanelli for their knowledge of Italy. Lisa Queen and Claire Wachtel for inspiration.

I
∞

When the phone call came in that morning, Patrizia Orman wasn't prepared. She was so busy acting nonchalant, even indifferent, as the German couple who'd wandered into the Holly Ardath Art Gallery for the third time that week circled around the painting, that she barely noticed Mona, the other gallery assistant, standing in front of her with a flustered look on her face. According to Patrizia's boss, the customer's third visit was do-or-die time. "If they come back twice, it doesn't really mean all that much," Holly had told her once. "But if they come back a third time, most likely the wife has dragged the husband along, and you've got yourself a sale. Unless they're neurotic, or really weird, or they don't have the money, they usually don't come back a fourth time."

"So what am I supposed to do in that situation?" Patrizia wanted to know.

Holly had smiled her mysterious, Zen-like smile.

"The hard sell never works," she said. "Let *them* be the ones who choose to part with fifty thousand dollars. Act like you've got better things to do, even if you don't."

The German couple seemed to be arguing about something, and as Holly had suggested, Patrizia wandered off, as if to examine some fascinating corner of the gallery she hadn't ever noticed before. At the same time she was alert to the slightest indication that the couple had made their final decision, whether it was a subtle shifting of the woman's chin, or a sign of fatigue or impatience in the man's expression. Ten minutes later the couple was still deep in conversation. Now the woman took a few hesitant steps backward, an affectionate frown on her face, as if she were imagining the painting on a living-room or dining-room wall thousands of miles away from New York. When the man began fidgeting with the heavy band of his gold watch, Patrizia came forward.

"May I get either of you an espresso, or a cappuccino? Or some sparkling water?"

The woman glanced up. She had dark, perfect skin and small, even white teeth, like the keys of a doll's piano. "The only thing that I want," she said to the man in a playful voice, ignoring Patrizia, "is this painting."

The German man was as chunky and graying as his wife was slender and youthful, and Patrizia had fantasized that he was a billionaire telecommunications mogul picking out a present for his fourth or fifth wife. "Okay," he said, nodding once. Okay: the international symbol of giving in, of agreeing to war, or to surrender, or in this case, to forking over nearly forty-five thousand dollars, including Patrizia's commission, not that she'd done very much, she reminded herself afterward, except pretend not to care. Patrizia was feeling buoyant—business was slow, and her last sale had taken place six months earlier—when Mona handed her the slip of pink paper and stood back, biting her lip hard, rocking a little on her heels, awaiting Patrizia's reaction as though it would decide her own.

"So we'll take it, then, eh?" the woman said to her husband. The German man grunted his assent, and when she turned to give him an embrace so intimate it was almost embarrassing, Patrizia took the opportunity to glance down at the note, and was startled to see a phone message received that morning from her godmother, Sarah Bogan.

Come home now. Mother seriously injured in car accident.

Days later Patrizia would remember only bits and pieces of that morning: the pain in her stomach, as though something had smacked her in the ribs, followed by the illogical impulse to telephone her mother—who else was she going to call?—and tell her the news. She remembered the expression on the face of the German couple, puzzlement giving way to compassion, and the German woman's hand on her shoulder. Outside, clutching her purse, Patrizia remembered being struck by the business-as-usual sounds and sights of Manhattan: a whiff of gasoline, a woman walking an over-weight dachshund, horns honking, spring sunlight, and the shadows crisscrossing the sidewalks of SoHo; struck, most of all, by how it made no sense whatsoever for bad things to happen on warm April days.

She remembered how at first the Pakistani taxi driver refused to take her to La Guardia. "I don't go to the air-ports," he announced when Patrizia scrambled into the backseat.

"Please, my mother was in an accident. She might be dying. You *have* to take me there."

The taxi driver must have heard the emotion in her voice, because he'd glanced at the beautiful, crying, dark-haired woman in the backseat, and shrugged. "Okay, miss," he said with a heavy sigh. "I have a mother, too. Put on your seat belt, I will get you there as fast as I can." And he'd raced her across town.

She would remember parts of the flight back to Illinois, as though it were happening to someone else, some shell-shocked twin who shared the same name as she: the patch-work quilt of the farms below her, a baby crying in the back row, the turbulence over Lake Erie, and how seeing the look on Patrizia's face, the stewardess, the one who was a dead ringer for Michelle Pfeiffer, handed her two bags of unsalted peanuts instead of one. Later she barely registered the shock of being back in her hometown of Argyle, Wisconsin, and how the swiftness of flying never really properly prepared you for being in one place in the morning and another place in the afternoon, or how she'd raced to the intensive-care unit of Carney Hospital, where her godmother embraced her in the fourth-floor hallway, her eyes red with crying. "I was visiting your mother for the past two days," Sarah said. "She was going to come back with me to Chicago for the weekend, we were going to go to the Degas show at the Art Institute, our cars were caravaning, and then this idiot truck—" Sarah Bogan searched Patrizia's face as though it held answers, though Sarah's own eyes said, only, *It's too late.*

What Patrizia did remember was one of the ICU nurses inquiring, in a weary, singsong voice, "Is there a husband here? Or a father?" Patrizia stared at her. "No," she replied, her voice breaking. "There are no fathers, there's only me," and then she collapsed onto the thin bed where Lizzie Orman's unfixable body lay, not moving.

She had never missed him, not really.

People asked her that now and again: what was it like growing up without a father? The answer Patrizia always gave was this: It was normal. How was she supposed to miss someone she'd never known? Never met? Someone whose face she knew only from two twenty-two-year-old photographs she hardly even looked at anymore?

It was like missing a city that didn't exist, a meal you hadn't even tasted, a view from a window it wasn't your place to look out of.

Which wasn't to say that over the years Patrizia hadn't been curious, or sad, or occasionally angry. Sometimes all three, like when birthdays and Christmases and Easters and New Years would slide by, and she wouldn't receive anything from him, not even a scrawled postcard, not that she'd expected to, really. Or the times she'd watched her mother scrambling to act as both mother and father on parents' days at school, at Patrizia's high-school graduation, and four years later, when she graduated from college. Those times Patrizia would tell herself that she was being sentimental and unrealistic. If she and her mother weren't embodying a tradition in the popular culture—mother, father, child—then at least they were embodying an honorable tradition in art. The greatest paintings of all time, after all, celebrated mothers and their children, not a father in sight.

But there were other times when Patrizia felt a longing for her father that frustrated her, since it wasn't at all specific. It was the presence of an absence, the acknowledgment of a part of her that was missing. It would have been so much easier if he were dead, but he wasn't. If he were dead, she could mourn the physical part of him that was lost forever, then close off forever the idea of ever seeing, or talking to, him again. But he wasn't dead, which meant that all her life Patrizia had held out the false hope of meeting him someday, somewhere, sometime.

"Do you think about your father ever?" a boyfriend had asked her once. Patrizia didn't give the true answer, which was, "All the time," but instead shrugged. "What's there to think about?"

Once, in art school, she had tried to paint a landscape from the window of her dormitory: a shelf of dogwood trees, and beyond them, a forest intercepted by a dirt road that ribboned out of sight behind a barn and a stack of newly cut lumber. The shadowy gray of the woods frustrated her; after two hours Patrizia still couldn't get the color right. She sanded, scraped off what she had done with her palette knife, then sanded again. Adding medium, she'd finally created the shade she wanted. She would always remember standing in her small studio in the thinning light of a late-autumn afternoon, gazing down at the palette with its array of smudged, runny colors, her thumb, strangely vulnerable, sticking up through the hole, and wishing her father could see what she'd done, could tell her that she'd gotten it *right*.

Over the years Patrizia had occasionally fantasized about meeting him. Finding out his address somehow, traveling to Europe and looking him up. In one of these fantasies, she showed up one day on his doorstep, ringing the buzzer, before the door opened finally. He would be an expatriate, living in London, in St. Johns Wood (she'd read somewhere once that this was where artsy people, painters and actors and writers and musicians, lived; it made sense that her father, an Italian art dealer, might have a place there, too). "Daddy," she would say; that was what she had always imagined she would call him—not "Dad," not "Pop" or "Pa," or "Father," but "Daddy"—and he'd stare at her for a long time, the words he wanted to say back failing him, knowing at once who she was: how could he not?

In another fantasy, he lived on a yacht in the south of France, and entertained lavishly; at night, they would watch fireworks off the bow. (Why would there be fireworks in the French sky? It didn't matter, the whole thing was made up, anyway.)

But in her most vivid fantasy, the one she returned to again and again, her father was living in a villa in Tuscany, or Umbria. He had a swimming pool surrounded by over-grown flowers that smelled sweet and heavy, like a liqueur. In the late afternoon, the pool water would turn to black marble, flecked with the bodies of a few insects. The meals would be prepared simply. There would be a white ham-mock and a housekeeper who didn't speak much English, but who smiled a lot at Patrizia. In the mornings, before it got too hot, Patrizia and her father would go for long walks together into the village, father and daughter, and on the way back, their bags would swing with the supplies they'd bought.

Occasionally, whenever she was in a strange city, Patri-zia would leaf through the local telephone directory. After all, her father might have moved to America without telling anyone. But she never found his name in any phone books, never even came close.

Returning home from these cities, Patrizia would feel adrift again, overwhelmed by the familiar feeling that she didn't belong anywhere. It was a feeling that had followed her for most of her life. Argyle, Wisconsin, the little suburb outside of Milwaukee where she'd been born and raised, didn't feel like home. Neither did California, where her mother had taken her to Disneyland one summer for her tenth birthday. Neither did Minnesota, where she'd attended art school, or even New York City, where two years earlier Patrizia had moved to pursue a career as a painter, despite her mother's repeated warnings that she would starve to death. So far she hadn't, though she'd come close a few times.

And it wasn't that her mother hadn't tried to make up for Patrizia's father not being around, either. For a long time Lizzie Orman fixated on all the most dire national statistics—that fatherless girls were more likely to drop out of high school, as well as more likely to get pregnant at an early age. She worried that Patrizia would fall prey to what happened to a lot of girls who didn't have fathers. When Patrizia was young, she'd lugged home caseloads of books about single parenting and only children. That was one of the benefits of working as a secretary in the psychology department of a huge Midwestern university: you had access to books and professors and sober-looking journals.

Once, in middle school, Patrizia had come home one day to find the ceiling above the kitchen table plastered with cutout, colored-in, taped-on planets, from the most massive, Jupiter, to the smallest, Pluto, as well as a stack of math and science textbooks, from basic algebra to cellular biology. Po-

litely, her mother had informed her that girls without fathers
tended to do worse at math and science than girls with fathers. "We're starting in on trig and the solar system today,"
she announced cheerfully. "Take a seat."

"I don't want you to grow up making men into leg-
endary figures," Lizzie told her when she was hitting ado-
lescence. "Because they're not. They're human. *Very*
human, in fact." She added, "Oh, and they're not *not* nec-
essary. I don't want you to make that mistake, either."

She brought up Masimilliano's name only occasionally.
The first time was when Patrizia had begun complaining
about her first name, how it set her apart from her friends,
and asked whether she couldn't change "Patrizia" to something, anything, else. To Patrizia's surprise, her mother
hadn't looked remotely sympathetic, or even amused. "Patrizia was the only name Masi and I could agree on for a
girl," she announced. "Boys' names were easy, girls' names
were a pain." A faint smile formed on her lips. "I don't think
I would ever forgive you if you changed your name to something more American." More than once she had told Patrizia
that she had inherited Masi's "killer looks"—the darkly
flashing eyes, the chestnut hair, the full lips, and (although
who knew what came from her side, and what came from
his?) a passion for art and painting.

Then there were the photographs. Faded, scuffed, their
colors garish in a mid-1970s way, their tops split with age
and handling. Two snapshots, like stills from some barely
remembered student-made movie, except these weren't

from a film, but from Patrizia's mother's life. One showed Patrizia's parents perched on the Spanish Steps in Rome, some faceless, passing tourist snapping their picture. Lizzie and Masimilliano—Masi, as he was known—were both twenty-two years old. Her mother was laughing behind oversized dark glasses; Masi had one hand posed with grave theatricality on one knee, as if in imitation of Rodin's famous sculpture *The Thinker*.

The other photograph was of Masi, by himself, taken from some distance away. He was standing beside an elaborate fountain, his dark hair tousled, his cracked leather jacket firmly zipped, both hands buried deep in his pockets. He looked faintly displeased about something—getting his picture taken most likely.

"What fountain is that?" Patrizia asked her mother once.

To her surprise, her mother frowned. "That's the Fontana dei Fiumi. It's in the Piazza Navona. It was designed by Bernini." She was silent. "At one time the Piazza Navona was my absolute favorite place in Rome. When I got there, it felt like the living, breathing embodiment of the city." "Why only once?" Patrizia asked. "Don't you still feel that way?" But her mother changed the subject.

In twenty-odd years, the photographs of Masi had never changed, though Patrizia had. As a child scanning the photos, not really understanding who she was looking at, she regarded this man, this Masimilliano, or Masi, as a stranger, interesting looking, charismatic even, but remote. Ten years later he was only a few years older than the boy at school

Patrizia had a crush on. At twenty-two, she examined the photos appraisingly, guiltily. Masi was exactly her age then. Would she ever be attracted to a man like that? Then the usual questions reasserted themselves: Where did Masi live? Was he married? Did he have a family of his own? Did she have any half sisters or brothers? Did he think about her ever?

"I don't think things will feel complete for you until you've made some kind of a peace with your father," Eric had told her the last time she'd seen him.

Patrizia had been involved with Eric Donovan off and on for the past few months, the latest in a succession of men she'd met since coming to New York. There was Richard, blond and eager looking, who over a series of romantic lunches told Patrizia everything, it seemed, about his life, except for the fact that he was married and the father of twins and that his wife was pregnant with their third child. Before Richard, there was Tom, who enjoyed a drink or two, until one morning he returned from the bathroom and curled up beside Patrizia with a freshly opened Heineken in his hand.

"You go for men who are unavailable for one reason or another," her mother told her bluntly. It was toward the end of their twice-weekly phone conversation, and Patrizia had just been describing a date she'd had with a man who still seemed to hold a torch for a former girlfriend.

"No, I don't," Patrizia replied. "I think I just have lousy taste in guys, that's all."

Her mother's voice was soothing. "I'm not saying I blame you, Patrizia. If the guys you go out with aren't available for whatever reason, well then, that means that if things don't work out between the two of you, it's no skin off your back, right? I think you pick the men you do in order to avoid getting hurt."

After they had hung up, Patrizia couldn't stop thinking about what her mother had said. It was true, she had never entirely trusted the male sex. She often found herself acting distantly and noncommittally when men were around, as if to keep them at arm's length. But Eric was kind and steady, a good listener, and he made her laugh. She had met him one day in late February when he had wandered into the Holly Ardath Gallery, announcing he was interested in the painting in the front window, an oil painting of animals playing under a white circus tent.

"How much is it anyway?" he asked, and when Patrizia quoted the price, Eric gazed at her humorously. "Hmm," he said, "Twenty-seven thousand dollars. Let me think about it for a second." After a beat, he glanced up brightly. "I just thought about it. If I sold my apartment, I could buy the painting, but then I'd have nowhere to hang it. So I guess there's no deal. But since I've just saved so much money, maybe I can buy you dinner?"

On their first night out, in a crowded Brazilian restaurant in the neighborhood where he lived, even before ordering, Eric gazed at Patrizia and said, "Just so you know, I was married once before and I have a daughter. She's six.

She means absolutely everything to me. All that means is that I'm not going to take you out dancing all night, because she's visiting me this week, and I promised the baby-sitter I'd be home by ten-thirty."

That night, they had exchanged all the relevant information of two people getting to know each other. Eric taught English at a private school on Manhattan's Upper East Side. He'd been married in his early twenties to his college sweetheart, but two years earlier they'd gotten divorced, and now they shared custody of their daughter, Katie. Surprised by how relaxed Eric made her feel, Patrizia realized that he was the first man she'd met in a while who'd really bothered to ask her about herself.

For the next hour and a half she told him about her life, growing up in the Midwest—the winters when the cold was sometimes so intense it felt hot, like dry ice, and fishermen drilled for perch and porgies on the frozen lakes—as well as about her mixed feelings about her hometown. "Sometimes I think a lot of people there believe they're not allowed to have opinions. But here"—Patrizia gestured at the tables around her, the handsomely dressed, chattering urban crowd—"I seem to spend most of my time defending my opinions." Over dessert, she told Eric about her mother, Lizzie, who'd been an art conservator in Italy before giving up her career to raise Patrizia. She told him about moving to New York with the intention of someday becoming an artist, but how the long hours she spent working at her gallery job left her very little time for anything else, and how she'd started getting up early in the morning to paint.

"And what about the name, please?" Eric asked at one point. "It sounds a little like one of Christopher Columbus's ships. The *Niña*, the *Pinta*, and the *Patrizia*."

"My father was Italian."

"Was? Is he living?"

"The last time I checked, he was." In response to Eric's confused expression, Patrizia added, "He's alive, as far as I know. I just—" She didn't finish. "He and I don't have a relationship. I've never even met him. My mom and he broke up before I was born."

"What was that like?" Eric liked to ask direct questions like that.

"Oh, it was excellent," she replied, trying to keep her voice from rising. "No male role models. I heartily recommend it."

"Do you miss having a father ever?"

There it was, the question again. "There's nothing to miss, Eric. He's irrelevant to my life. He's totally useless."

Eric stared at her, openmouthed. "Oh my God, you mean that fathers are useless? I'm so glad you told me before I wasted any more time with my daughter."

"I'm not saying that, Eric. Believe me, not all fathers are like mine."

"Speaking of daughters . . ." Eric excused himself to telephone home, and when he came back to the table, he was smiling. "Katie says to say hello. She wants to know if you like tights. I told her I didn't think you were wearing any, but I was pretty sure you had a few pairs in your drawer at home."

Later the two of them walked home through the crowded Manhattan streets in near silence. It was the end of winter, and the streets were shiny with sleet, traffic reduced to a gleaming, honking standstill. "So what's it like for you, having a daughter?" Patrizia asked at one point.

She could hear the awkwardness in her voice, and despised it, but Eric didn't seem to notice. "They're tough as nails," he replied with a laugh. "Maybe because they have to be. But I'll tell you, I *love* having a girl. No matter what they say, they *are* different." He stopped to stare earnestly at her. "Let me give you an example. I didn't want to be accused of being a chauvinist, so last year I gave Katie a toy truck for her birthday. The next thing I knew she'd wrapped a blanket around it and pretended it was a *baby truck*. Then she gave the truck a *bottle*. I mean, what was I going to say?"

Eric hesitated in front of Patrizia's apartment building. "Doesn't your door have a downstairs lock?" he asked.

"It keeps on breaking," Patrizia explained. Since arriving in New York City, she'd lived in the far East Village, on Avenue D, in a dilapidated fourth-floor walk-up across the street from a garage and a dry cleaner. "If I lived any farther east," she liked to joke to her friends, "I'd probably be floating in the East River." In an attempt to spruce up Patrizia's building, the landlord had painted the lobby and the interior a fluorescent pink, but that still didn't conceal its age and decrepitude, and it certainly didn't justify the high rent, which Patrizia split down the middle with her roommate, Lucy, an aspiring actress. When she'd first come to New York, Patrizia had found the building and the neighborhood appealing, but more and more she found herself dreading coming home at night to the clinking pipes and the thickly overpainted radiators, the noisy rooster across the air shaft that someone kept as a pet, and Lucy, who spent most of the time auditioning for parts she didn't get, and the rest of the time drinking coffee and smoking Russian cigarettes and poring over *Backstage*. "Kind of different from where you live, huh?"

Eric lived in a huge rent-stabilized apartment that he had taken over from his grandmother when she died. It was on the Upper East Side, a few blocks from the school where he taught, and close to a park where he and Katie liked to go Roller Blading. "I want you to be safe, that's all," he said.

"I can take care of myself, Eric," Patrizia replied lightly. "I always have."

Patrizia saw Eric three or four more times over the next several weeks. She could see that he was falling in love with her—he had told her as much—but the more he pursued her, the more she resisted him. Increasingly, she'd come to think of Eric as an adorable older brother—funny, rumpled, protective—rather than as a boyfriend. Still, there was no denying that his steadiness came as a comfort to her after the unpredictability of the other men she'd met since arriving in New York.

A few weeks after their first meeting, Patrizia met Eric's daughter, Katie, for the first time. Katie was a small, blond, energetic girl with penetrating blue eyes, and as the three of them made their way to a pizza parlor in Chelsea, Katie insisted that she walk between Eric and Patrizia, and that on a count of three, they swing her forward and upward until her feet left the ground, ". . . without letting go, okay, you guys?"

Eric and Patrizia played this game all the way to the restaurant, Patrizia feeling her grip grow more uncertain as she was overcome with feelings that confused and embarrassed her—a combination of maternal warmth for Eric's daughter, mixed with a strange resentment that no mother and father walking together side by side on a street had ever done this for her. She felt cheated. At the same time she was frustrated with longing, especially when they entered the restaurant, and Katie let go of Patrizia's hand but held on to her father's.

"I hope that you notice all these 'awwww' expressions that I'm getting from the women in this restaurant," Eric remarked when their dinner arrived. "Women are suckers for fathers and daughters together."

"Maybe because it's so unbelievably rare," Patrizia said sharply.

Eric touched his hand to hers. "Oh, come on, fathers

aren't as bad as all that." A moment later he sent Katie over to a small deck where kids could watch the white-hatted cooks in the fiery kitchen flipping pizzas into the air and catching them again. When she was gone, Eric turned to Patrizia. "Look, Patrizia," he said. "My own father wasn't all that warm a guy." His father, a banker, didn't know how to be, he went on, though Eric could see in his eyes sometimes that he wanted to hug his son, or kiss him good night. "When I was four years old, he started shaking hands with me before I went to bed," Eric recalled. "It was like he was shaking hands with one of his clients." He was silent. "But when my dad died, I cried and cried. It wasn't just that I missed him, it was that he and I had missed out on an incredible relationship. You know, you can have all the father figures you want in this life, but you only have one father."

Later that night Eric and Patrizia walked uptown along Fifth Avenue in the direction of Eric's apartment while Katie skipped ahead, checking out the window displays in the Midtown department stores. It was snowing lightly, and New York was at its most appealing.

"I've been thinking about what fathers give to girls," Eric remarked. "There's this old line I read somewhere once. 'Mothers give you roots and fathers give you wings.' I liked that for some reason."

"It sounds like something you'd read on the back of a tea bag in a Chinese restaurant," Patrizia said coolly.

Eric ignored her cynicism. "Never disdain the wisdom of tea bags!" he crowed, adding, this time more seriously,

"I just know that I try and be the best person around I can be for Katie. I want her to know that I'll be there for her whenever, forever. That I'll support her in whatever she does. All she has to do is call me, and I'll be there."

At the entrance to his apartment building, he hesitated. "Do you want to come over later? I've just got to put you-know-who into bed, but after that I'm free."

Patrizia had spent the night with Eric several times already, after making certain Katie was sound asleep, and when they were in bed together, her doubts about him fell away despite herself. Still, afterward, she felt as though something crucial were missing: true desire, maybe, or was it simply a sense of mystery? That night, Patrizia found she wasn't in the mood for Eric's drafty apartment, or for his tender but predictable lovemaking, or for getting up at dawn to go home and change before reporting to work at the gallery. "I have to get up early," she lied. "But thanks all the same."

Katie was already in the lobby, showing the doorman the wad of uncooked pizza dough she had gotten at the restaurant. "You know something?" Eric said at last. "I'm not going to give up on you that easily."

"I don't know what you're talking about—" Patrizia started to say.

"You're doing a really good job of pushing me away." When she began to protest, he held a finger to her mouth. "Don't worry, I don't take it personally. I have a feeling it may be something you do as far as men are concerned. So what's the longest you've ever had a relationship with some-body? Can I guess? Two weeks? Three weeks?"

"That's actually none of your business," Patrizia said.

"Can I say one more thing, and you won't think I'm being totally out of line?"

It was then that Eric had said what he'd said, words that remained in Patrizia's head, like an uneven melody, for days afterward: *I don't think things will feel complete for you until you've made some kind of peace with your father.*

Patrizia had stared back at him, stunned. "Why do you think you know the first thing about it?"

Eric bowed slightly. It was part apology, part wise man. "All I know is exactly what you've told me, mixed with what I see when I'm around you. And I wasn't a psych major in college for nothing."

"You think I should get in touch with my father?" She couldn't keep the sarcasm out of her voice. " 'Hey, Dad, remember me? Your daughter? Want to have a cup of coffee and a doughnut? Want to reject me again?' " Her voice returned to normal. "Not that it's any of your business what-soever, but I *have* made peace with my father, as you say. He's a deadbeat. He's never been a part of my life, and he never will be if I have anything to do with it. End of story." She turned to go.

"Well, guess what? I'm not your father," Eric called after her. "And you're not your mother, either."

"What's that supposed to mean?"

"Think about it, Patrizia."

"Why don't you mind your own business, Eric," Patrizia replied coolly. "This isn't Psych 101, and I'm not your patient."

"Patrizia—" he started to protest.

She couldn't hear what he said next as she stormed down the street, past the newspaper kiosk on the corner, past the shuttered boutiques and the movie theater letting out its final show, and onto Lexington Avenue. She didn't hear what Eric called after her, and no matter what it was, she would have done the same thing: walk away.

Lizzie Orman's memorial service was held on an overcast Friday afternoon, and was attended mostly by members of the university department—faculty, students, secretaries. Afterward, there was a small reception at Patrizia's old childhood house, where Patrizia stood by the door, accepting the sympathy and embraces of well-wishers. By mid-afternoon, when the sun broke through the clouds, everybody had cleared out of the house except for Patrizia and Sarah Bogan, her godmother, who'd spent the past few days sleeping in the guest bedroom, dealing with the telephone and the doorbell, fielding the arrival of neighbors and acquaintances bearing foil-covered meals, and generally helping Patrizia out.

It was Patrizia's first real experience with death, and it was true what they said: something left the body. Maybe it wasn't a soul, or a spirit, but it was something. Gazing down at her mother's face in the hospital, she'd watched it, whatever that thing was, loosen, then drift upward, finally taking leave. A moment later Patrizia would swear to herself that nothing at all had just happened. But when she glanced back down, her mother's face seemed subtly different. Occupied these past few years with worry, with phone and electricity and mortgage payments, working overtime and sometimes on the weekends at a job she didn't particularly like, spending all day staring at the skim-milk blue of her computer screen—now that familiar face had softened again, and turned youthful. In death, Lizzie Orman had become a girl of twenty-two again.

To Patrizia it didn't seem right that in the days following the service, things went on as usual. People who had never known of her mother's birth, much less of her death, continued living their lives, showing up at work, meeting after work for drinks, taking the dog to the vet, planning birthdays, holidays, anniversaries. Cars backed out of driveways in the morning and came back before dinner; the sun rose and fell; airplanes took off and landed on schedule. The notice in the local newspaper made no mention of the kind of person her mother was. No mention of any of the things she loved—Renoir's paintings, spending all day at the Art Institute of Chicago, the smell in the air right after it rained, a fire in the fireplace even when the weather wasn't really cold enough for a fire, garlic mashed potatoes, Mozart, Cape Cod potato chips, anything having to do with Italy—or the things she didn't love as much—rudeness, crowds, loafers with tassels on them, bumper stickers, tofu, flying. Just the date of her birth and her death, a summary of where she worked, and the name of her only immediate survivor: Patrizia.

On the day of the memorial service, the red light on Lizzie Orman's answering machine in the downstairs hallway was blinking frantically, like a distress signal. Among the messages from her mother's friends and colleagues was one from Patrizia's roommate, Lucy. "Eric called," Lucy announced in her breathy, theatrical voice. "He hadn't heard about your mom, so I told him. I hope you don't mind that I gave him this number." Two messages later Patrizia heard Eric's voice. "Patrizia, I'm here if you need me," he said, almost sadly. "All you have to do is call me, and I'll be there." But preoccupied by the world of her mother, which she had left behind when she moved to New York, Patrizia hadn't called him back.

Instead, she spent the next week dealing with her mother's belongings. At her godmother's suggestion, Patrizia had placed a lot of things in storage until she knew what she wanted to do with them. "You're still in shock," Sarah told her gently after the memorial service. "I know you probably don't feel that way, but you are. Someday you'll look back at this time, and say to yourself, 'I thought I was in control but I was just going through the motions.'"

The first few days were the hardest, particularly when Patrizia learned the details of the car accident. It had taken place on a highway some twenty miles north of Chicago.

The last vestiges of that winter's snowfall were melting, caus-
ing a thick fog to rise off the plains and the freeways, and
according to the police report, the driver in the truck in
front of Patrizia's mother's car had slammed on his brakes
to avoid hitting a car that had merged onto the highway.
Lizzie hadn't been able to stop in time, and her rusty Honda
Accord had smashed into the back of the truck, then flipped
over. Sarah, who was following several cars behind, had
been able to jam on her brakes just in time. "I told her we
should have driven in the same car to save gas," Sarah said
to Patrizia softly, "but your mother told me she was listening
to a book on tape she liked, that she knew I would hate,
and she wanted to finish it."

Following the service, Sarah had suggested that Patrizia
take a room at the Days Inn several blocks from the house,
but Patrizia had shaken her head stubbornly no. "I insist,"
said Sarah, adding, "it's my treat," but Patrizia wouldn't
budge. The silence of her mother's house, the house where
she had spent her first eighteen years, intrigued her more
than it frightened her. That first night following the funeral,
she wandered from room to room, surrounded by the evidence of a life that was being lived until suddenly it had
been interrupted, cut off. There was the plate lying in the
sink on which her mother had eaten her breakfast that morning, the empty strawberry yogurt container, the bed left un-
made upstairs, the book half-read on the bedside table, even
her mother's fingerprints in a jar of cold cream. Patrizia had
climbed into that bed, which still smelled like her mother,

and hugged the still-warm pillow for a long time, until she'd fallen asleep herself.

"You're the only person I have left," Patrizia said to her godmother a few days later as they were packing up the dining room.

Sarah Bogan was her mother's closest childhood friend, both of them the products of large Midwestern families, though Sarah was an only child, and Lizzie had been the only girl in an extended family of brothers and sisters. When Lizzie had gone off the Europe to study art conservation, Sarah had followed convention, attending Smith College in Massachusetts, and afterward marrying one of the most eligible bachelors in Chicago. When Patrizia was born, Lizzie hadn't had to think twice to ask Sarah to be her daughter's godmother, and her oldest friend was honored. It was Sarah who had arranged for close friends to host Patrizia in their massive East Side apartment when Patrizia had first arrived in New York; and it was Sarah who'd managed to get her an interview at the Holly Ardath Gallery when the personnel director there had told Patrizia that there were no jobs available "but we'll certainly take down your name."

Now again it was Sarah who was helping Patrizia clear out her mother's house, the dishes and saucers and glasses and cups and silverware from the kitchen drawers and cabinets; the contents of the bathroom, the living room, and the upstairs hallway, the piles of books from the overflowing bookcases, the boxes of records neither Patrizia nor her mother played anymore, but couldn't bear to throw away;

all the accumulations of a lifetime, now placed in cardboard boxes marked KITCH. And MISC. DINING ROOM and KNICKKNACKS, LIV. ROOM. And it was Sarah who'd gone to the First Union Savings Bank to clear out Lizzie's small safe-deposit box.

Now Sarah glanced up. "That's not true that I'm the only person you have left, Patrizia," she said quietly. "Nobody is all by themselves, ever. You have your cousins, your uncle, you have all your friends."

Sarah's husband, Patrizia's uncle Bill, was a successful futures trader who was seldom at home, tending instead to his many properties around the country, including ranches in Wyoming and Texas. To Patrizia, Uncle Bill had always been a distant, preoccupied figure, with no real understanding or love of children, and she hardly knew him.

"I meant . . ." but Patrizia's voice trailed off.

"I know what you meant." Sarah had always been able to read Patrizia's mind, to finish her sentences for her, though this time the meaning was fairly obvious: Patrizia had no immediate family left in the world. Sarah seemed to be gazing off at a point beyond her goddaughter's shoulders, and at last, when she spoke, her voice was flat and somewhat brittle. "You know, Patrizia, you may think you're all alone in the world, but you're not. Not by a long shot."

"What do you mean?"

Sarah hesitated, and then, seemingly resigned to what she was about to do, she finished packing the carton of Christmas ornaments and rose up to her full height. Crossing the room, she paused at the couch where earlier she'd tossed her coat, and from under it, she pulled out a worn red duffel bag. "Here's what was in the safe-deposit box," she said, handing the bag to Patrizia, "for better or for worse. And God help me if this is the wrong thing to do, but I think probably by now you're old enough to know."

"To know what?"

Sarah indicated with a slight nod of her head that Patrizia should open the duffel bag.

"To know what?" Patrizia repeated, and when Sarah didn't answer, she undid first the snaps and then the zipper. The bag, or its contents, smelled musky though not unpleasant, as though it had been sitting for years collecting dust and moisture not in an airtight safe-deposit box, but in an attic or a basement. A moment later Patrizia pulled out a passport and a necklace. Two curling stock certificates, which made her smile despite herself. Five years earlier her mother had joined an all-women's investing club, and placed a small amount of money in a pharmaceutical company that she claimed she had "a very strong feeling about." Since then the stock had plummeted, losing most of its value. It was a running joke between the two of them, Patrizia inquiring about how her mother's single stock was doing, and Lizzie replying, invariably, "You just wait, your mother will be a mogul yet."

Aside from a bunch of letters at the bottom of the bag, the duffel was empty. The letters were bound tightly with two cheerful rubber bands, one red and one green. There must have been two dozen of them, ranging from the tissuelike robin's-egg blue of aerograms to several plain white no-nonsense business-size letters. But what first first caught Patrizia's attention were the stamps, with their unfamiliar images and dense, curling writing.

"What are all these?" she asked finally.

Many of the blue aerograms were torn, she noticed, as though they'd been slit open roughly or hurriedly, or in anger; others looked as though they had never been opened.

Patrizia knew immediately whom they were all from.

She was barely aware of Sarah's voice telling her, with the utmost gentleness and respect, "Read one."

A moment later Patrizia picked up the blue aerogram on top of the pile. The check fell out before she realized it was there, fluttering to the ground and landing faceup on the rug beneath the coffee table. The crude black-ink handwriting, smeared in places, riveted her. The sevens were crossed, presumably to distinguish them from—what? And then she noticed the date.

"This was mailed ten years ago," Patrizia said, trying to keep her voice steady. She opened up another aerogram, this one addressed to her mother, sealed—for that matter, never opened. Careful not to tear the fragile paper, she slit one side with her fingernail, and when she did, another gauzy blue-green check dropped out into her lap, this one dated five years earlier.

Five years ago. Patrizia would have been just eighteen, barely able to afford art supplies, her art-school education

financed by a home equity loan her mother had taken out
against the value of her house. Patrizia had a sudden image
of herself waitressing off campus at a restaurant called The
Heart and Ladle, forced to wear a frilly uniform and cap,
contributing her meager salary to skinny Windsor & New-
ton oil and watercolor brushes, another year in which her
mother went on no vacations, and treated herself to nothing
at all.

Another aerogram, and another check, this one dated
fifteen years earlier. Fifteen years ago Patrizia would have
been eight years old, sitting with her mother on a pullout
folding chair at her school's parents' day while around her
classmates chattered laughingly and easily with both their
parents. In the winter, her mother would have covered the
windows with plastic sheeting to keep the electricity bills
down, and made frequent trips to the cooperative farm two
towns away to get cheap fruits and vegetables.

The numbers scrawled on the checks were equally stag-
gering. Two thousand dollars. Five thousand dollars. One
for ten thousand dollars. None of the checks had been
cashed, or from the looks of it, even handled by human
hands. In fact, as far as Patrizia could tell, when the aerograms and letters had arrived, her mother had either opened
them, scanned them, and put them aside, or in most cases
refused to open them at all, simply tossing them all into the
duffel bag. She had never once mentioned any of the letters
to Patrizia.

Sarah's voice had taken on a searching, apologetic quality. "Your mom . . . over the years . . . of course the money would have helped, but . . . principle of the thing . . . she didn't want anything to do with him, and I can't really blame her . . . though I told her, Liz, these checks and letters, they aren't for you, they're for Patrizia."

From where she was sitting, Patrizia was aware of the black plastic tail of her mother's corny old Felix the Cat clock swinging back and forth above the living-room couch, and of the refrigerator humming in the kitchen. Her mother's life, limited by no money, no means of escape, seemed courageous to her all of a sudden. She thought back on all their cost cutting over the years, the carefully scissored-out coupons in a neat stack next to the kitchen phone, the boiler in the basement that had to be tinkered with whenever anybody took a shower longer than five minutes, her mother driving the same old broken-down Honda Accord year after year, even though it had a small jagged hole on the floor of the passenger side where you could see the stripes of the road underneath you. "Why?" Patrizia asked finally, faintly. "I don't understand this at all. Why?"

Sarah gazed down at her, idly moist-eyed, for a few moments. "Oh boy," she said. "Talk about opening up a can of worms. Was I wrong showing these to you?"

Slowly, as if in a trance, Patrizia shook her head. "No," she said at last, her mouth dry, "I'm actually glad that you did."

Sarah extracted a Kleenex from her purse and blew her

nose discreetly. "So I'm guessing she never told you anything."

"About what?"

"About her and Masi."

Patrizia was surprised by the casualness with which Sarah uttered his name. Masi: as though she'd been saying it all her life. Who else knew about this man? Had Patrizia deliberately, for some reason, been kept in the dark? "No," she said honestly. "She never told me anything."

"You're kidding, right?"

"Why would I be kidding?" Her mother had always been unusually silent about the topic of Patrizia's father, shrugging off questions with, "Honey, that was so long ago. I wish I had the memory of an elephant, but I don't." Another time she'd said, in a subdued tone, "I will never speak badly of your father, in the same way that I hope that he never speaks badly of me."

"Do you know why Lizzie—I mean, your mother—left him?"

"Geography," Patrizia replied softly, though she'd always sensed this wasn't the whole truth, that this just couldn't be possible. "She wanted to come back to live in America, and he didn't."

"That's what she told you?"

"Yes." Patrizia was starting to feel agitated, uncomfortable.

"So you're telling me you don't know anything else

about him? What he's like, what he does for a living, anything?"

"She never talked about him." Masi. Her father. "I know that he's an art dealer somewhere."

"Yes, Rome." Sarah hesitated. "And you never asked her more?"

"Every time I tried to bring up the subject, she would say that things hadn't worked out between them." Tiredly, Patrizia added, "Oh, and for reasons of his own he decided not to stay in touch." Then: "It sounds stupid just to—"

"So do you want to know the truth, Patrizia? Would it make a difference to you if you knew the truth? Do you want to know?"

"Yes." Patrizia could barely hear her own voice in the room, adding, faintly, "I *do* want to know," and she took a seat on the couch now, carefully, waiting.

2
∞

What Lizzie Orman noticed first were the *gatti*.

There were cats everywhere in Rome—sunning themselves on stoops, darting in and out of the Forum, or the Colosseum, and lounging in crumbling squares where the emperor Augustus had probably once addressed a multitude of cheering Romans. Almost every afternoon, as she walked back to her apartment on the Via dei Pettinari, she passed someone, usually an old woman, crouched on the sidewalk, her skirts parachuting blackly around her, setting out the remnants of her own dinner in a shallow bowl for a group of shyly hungry cats. They were Italian cats, Lizzie said to herself wryly—no doubt they spoke better Italian than she did. Then again, after almost a year in Rome, she noticed that just about everybody, including the children, was fluent in a language that in person seemed to have little in common with the Italian she'd studied in college.

Her parents had been unhappy when she told them she wanted to go to Italy to study art conservation. "What about a state school near us?" her father inquired. At the time Lizzie knew that he was worried about whether or not he could afford to send her abroad—he was a regional salesman at a furniture factory—but he didn't want to come out and say it.

"Dad, it's a state-run program," Lizzie explained gently. "It's free for Italians, and *practically* free for Americans." Realizing he was still reluctant, she drew out her final ammunition. "Plus, you've always told me that someone who majored in studio art in college has no job skills to speak of, and now finally I think I've found something I could be really good at."

Her father didn't answer, but instead merely gazed down at the television listings of his newspaper.

"Dad, I only type two and a half words a minute," Lizzie went on, adding, almost desperately, "and that's when I'm on a roll."

Even though in the end her father had supported her decision to study in Rome, the expression on his face that night saddened Lizzie. She knew that he'd counted on all his children living near him for the rest of their lives, but it wasn't working out that way. Her two brothers and one sister had either already left the rural town of Argyle, Wisconsin—population 14,000—or else were planning to. Two months earlier her sister had accepted a computer software job on the West Coast, and recently one of her brothers, fearful of the draft, had announced that he was moving to Canada. Her other brother had lived and worked in Louisiana for several years now. Her father's children were leaving, setting forth into the world, and even though this was what children had done for generations, Lizzie couldn't help but feel a tug in her stomach on her father's behalf, especially since as the youngest, she knew she'd always been his favorite. Impulsively, she kissed him on the forehead. "Daddy, I can't live at home forever," she said quietly.

"I'm not asking you to stay here forever," he replied gruffly. "Just until you're fifty," he added, and he turned away so she couldn't see that his eyes were shiny with tears.

For as far back as she could remember, Lizzie Orman had wanted to be a painter. As a girl, she'd been obsessed with the lives of great painters—Van Gogh, Monet, Cézanne, Matisse, Rembrandt, and her favorite, Auguste Renoir. She could even recite the colors of Renoir's palette, and what paintbrushes he used. The colors: silver white, chrome yellow, Naples yellow, ocher, raw sienna, vermilion, rose lake, Veronese green, viridian, cobalt blue, ultramarine blue. The brushes: flat silk, as well as ones made of marten hair. On the rare occasions when her family made the nearly two-hour drive south to Chicago, Lizzie would drag her mother to the Art Institute, while her father, who always protested, "Art isn't my thing," stayed in their crowded hotel room, baby-sitting her brothers and sister.

By age sixteen, Lizzie knew that what she wanted more than anything was to devote her life to art, and to painting. She also knew that it was doubtful that her parents would approve of her ambitions. A girl from a good middle-class Midwestern family was supposed to marry as soon as possible, set up a good house for her husband, raise well-mannered children, and perhaps, if there was any time left over, work part-time in a volunteer job. Painting was just too quirky, too unstable a profession, for a young woman to pursue.

As a result, Lizzie had learned to keep her love of painting a secret. Her early attempts at drawing—the spindly legs of her parents' kitchen table, her brother's navy-blue sweatpants draped across the top of the chair in his bedroom—were done in private, the sketch pad concealed in her lap, the charcoal clenched in her hand like a secret weapon. If anybody asked her what she was doing, she would close her pad, smile sweetly, and say, "Nothing. Why, what are *you* doing?"

Finally her mother approached her as Lizzie was heading off to school one morning. "Lizzie," she said, "there's no party line that says you have to be conventional." Lizzie stared back at her mother, not understanding, and then her mother told her that long ago she had wanted to be a writer, that she had written short stories all through her teens, and later, articles for her college magazine. "But I stopped. I got married. I told myself I didn't have the time, I was a housewife with four children underfoot. But the truth of the matter is I didn't *make* the time." Her mother's eyes were kind. "I love my life, but please don't allow what I let happen to me happen to you. Take a risk. Dare to be different." She stuffed a crumpled twenty-dollar bill into Lizzie's lapel pocket. "And for heaven's sakes, go out and get yourself a decent drawing pad."

It wasn't until she reached college age that Lizzie realized that if she were to become a painter, she would have to leave the Midwest. She loved her hometown—the farms and the lakes and the cornfields and, in the winters, the lake waves frozen and shimmering in mid-crest under the January sunlight like unfinished sculptures—but she also knew that the Midwest was no place to pursue a serious career in art. She wanted to paint scenes she loved and remembered from her hometown—but to do that, she couldn't live there.

In the fall semester of her senior year in college, Lizzie attended a lecture given by an art conservator visiting from the Museum of Fine Arts in Boston. Expecting to be bored, she instead found herself enthralled by the conservator's detailed descriptions of how she had helped to restore *Carmelina,* one of Matisse's later paintings. Approaching the podium after class, Lizzie blurted out, "How can I learn how to do what you do?" The conservator laughed, and then to Lizzie's amazement, suggested that Lizzie drop by the hotel where she was staying so the two of them could discuss it further.

The conservator was waiting for her in the downstairs lobby of the hotel when Lizzie showed up, and after making small talk for a few minutes, the older woman turned to her. "Are you a painter yourself?" When Lizzie admitted that she was, the conservator took out of her purse a dark red swatch, a tablet, and a small watercolor set. She pointed to the swatch. "Okay, see if you can re-create that color."

It took Lizzie a while, but eventually she'd managed to create the precise color of the red swatch. The older woman didn't take her eyes off her for one second, focusing back and forth between Lizzie's hands and Lizzie's eyes and the supple working relationship between the two. "I'm very impressed" was all she said when Lizzie was finished. "It takes most people an hour on their first try."

The older woman went on to explain that becoming an art conservator was extremely hard work, that you couldn't become a conservator unless you were an artist yourself, that conservation entailed an enormous amount of study—not just art history and drawing technique, but advanced chemistry—and above all, extraordinary patience.

"If you are still interested," the woman concluded nearly two hours later, "I would advise you to go to study in Italy. They will teach you things there that you will not be taught anywhere else in the world." With a small smile, she added, "For better or for worse."

"How do I find out about studying in Italy?" Lizzie asked.

"I'll help you, that's how."

Several days later, when the official application to the Istituto Centrale del Restauro in Rome arrived in her family's mail from the Italian consulate in New York, Lizzie filled it out and waited, rushing home almost daily during lunchtime from her job at a local real-estate office to see if the Istituto had come to any decision. A few weeks later, when she learned she had been accepted, and not only that, but that classes were to begin almost immediately, she was overjoyed, though for her parents' sake, she went out of her way not to show it.

At the airport terminal, as various flight announcements blared over the loudspeakers, Lizzie's father hugged her good-bye, then held her shoulders gravely with both hands. "I just want you to know that you make me so proud," he said. "I know that for Mom's and my sake, you've been trying to keep a lid on all your excitement, but Jesus, this is the big time! Go for it, and don't ever look back!"

Lizzie's first few months in Rome were a blur of confusion, excitement, and chronic embarrassment. Over and over again, she heard herself say, *"Mi dispiace"* and *"Scusi"*— I'm sorry, I'm sorry—at coffee shops, in restaurants, in museums, in churches, wherever it was possible to mismanage or mangle the Italian language. All the courses at the Istituto were conducted entirely in Italian, and for the first six months Lizzie could barely follow what her professors were saying. Through a local English-speaking newspaper, she found a cheap two-bedroom apartment along the Via dei Pettinari, which she shared with a fellow student from the Istituto, a fashionable, dark-haired woman from Milan named Donatella.

During Lizzie's first few months in Rome it was Donatella who acted as her unofficial chaperon, taking Lizzie to the Borghese Galleries and to the Piazza di Spagna, and then to the elegant shops along the Via Condotti and the Via Veneto, stopping afterward for cappuccinos at the famous Babington's Tea Rooms. Under Donatella's wing, Lizzie visited St. Peter's Cathedral, joining the crush of tourists staring up at the ceiling of the Sistine Chapel. Later Donatella introduced her to the Palazzo dei Conservatori, where the two women gazed at paintings and murals by Veronese, Tintoretto, Rubens, and Titian, and to the Church of the Gesù, where Lizzie marveled at the magnificent frescoes. Together, they explored different sections of Rome. One week, they explored the Palatine; the next, the Aventine; the next, Janiculum; the following week, the Campo dei Fiori, a huge open-air fruit-and-vegetable market, where elderly Italian women sat crouched atop overturned buckets, peeling artichokes, and where the dark statue of Giordano Bruno stared down at all the commotion.

"Who is this guy Giordano Bruno? And why does he look so angry at the world?" Lizzie shouted to Donatella, trying to be heard over the sound of Romans haggling over the prices of lemons, cherries, mushrooms, and fresh fish.

Donatella explained that Giordano Bruno was a Renaissance philosopher and writer whose books had come under attack by authorities during the Inquisition. "He was thrown in prison for seven years, then when he was let out, he was taken to the Campo dei Fiori, bound and gagged, and burned at the stake," Donatella replied cheerfully. "If that had happened to you, I'll bet you wouldn't look all that pleased either."

It was also Donatella who instructed Lizzie in the day-to-day workings of Rome: how to buy *francobolli*—postage stamps—as well as a monthly bus pass at the *tabaccaio,* where to find the best fresh strawberries (the stalls along the Via Portuense), the name of the small pastry shop where Lizzie could find a type of cannoli that Donatella swore was like dying and going to heaven. Though Donatella had warned her about Italy's famously tangled bureaucracy, Lizzie was still flabbergasted to learn she had to wait six months to get a telephone installed in their apartment. Once, when she found herself losing steam before her afternoon class at the Istituto and asked Donatella where she could find a cup of coffee to go, Donatella explained that in Italy, there was no such thing as "coffee to go," or for that matter, "fast food." She marched Lizzie down to a coffee shop, planted her at the counter, ordered them both shots of espresso, and started to explain that Romans took their meals seriously, and didn't rush through them. Where was the pleasure in grabbing a Styrofoam cup of coffee, gulping it down, and barely tasting it? Meals were an occasion for appreciation and gratitude, not to mention good conversation. And Lizzie already knew that Romans typically liked to shop for food on the day they planned to eat it. "Our country has known war," Donatella told her with a shrug, "unlike your own. We have known what it's like not to have enough. Every day we are careful with what we have, because the older ones remember that all of it can be taken away."

Following an unfortunate encounter Lizzie had with a man on a Roman bus, it was Donatella who sat her down and told her which city buses to take and which to avoid, since certain bus lines were notorious for pickpockets and overly familiar men. "Unless it is something you enjoy, which I somehow doubt very much, you should stay away from the buses where men pinch your behind and squeeze your breasts," Donatella advised. "I had been pinched—and worse—by more strangers on buses in this city than I can tell you before I learned that I have a better left hook than I thought."

Over time, though, Lizzie had mastered the bus system. She now knew the best place to get her laundry done—the *tintoria* on the Via dei Fori Imperiali, though usually, to save money, she would wash her clothing in her apartment's tiny washer and hang it up to dry wherever she could find space. After several aborted attempts, she'd learned how to use a public pay phone, and discovered, too, that there were mandatory dress codes inside most Roman churches, that men and women both were expected to cover their bare arms and torsos. One of the happiest days of her life was when an Italian woman asked her for directions to Rome's central train station, the Stazione Termini, and Lizzie was able to tell her the precise route to take, and in unbroken Italian, too.

The classes at the Istituto were another matter. Once,

during her first month, Lizzie made the mistake of referring to herself as a student of art restoration, and her *professori* sternly corrected her that she, Lizzie, was studying to become an art *conservator*, not an art *restorer*. *Restorer* implied that you were maybe doing something you shouldn't, altering and maybe even destroying an artist's original vision. *Conservation* was the proper word, in the sense that you were conserving—and thus respecting, and honoring—the artist's original intention. And the Italians, Lizzie found out, used conservation methods and techniques that hadn't changed in, well, since the beginning of time.

For example, to bolster old paintings whose canvases were deteriorating, American conservators used a synthetic adhesive to attach a second piece of fabric to the first. In Italy, Lizzie spent two months learning how to mix, and then apply, a sticky paste, which had to be done with the utmost care. When Italians cleaned a painting, they believed that it was best to leave a little bit of wear and tear behind, a slight film of dirt, a *patina,* as they kept calling it (*la patina* seemed to be the favorite word of most of Lizzie's teachers). This was different from American and English conservators, who cleaned, in the words of one of her *professori,* "like a bunch of obsessive-compulsive housewives."

Early on, Lizzie had discovered to her surprise that she was the only American studying at the Istituto; there were students from Scandinavia, England, Austria, Switzerland, and Eastern Europe, but most of her fellow classmates were Italian. As if to initiate her into the ways of their country, they had taken to calling Lizzie "Betta," short for "Elisa-betta."

The days at the Istituto followed a pattern that seldom varied from week to week, and from month to month. Mornings were filled with classes in art history, chemistry, and drawing technique, and afterward, the students were permitted a late-morning recess. Then Lizzie and her class-mates repaired to a neighborhood coffee shop, leaning up against the counter and drinking small, strong cups of es-presso, snacking on thin slices of *pizza bianca,* and smoking Marlboros (to her dismay, Lizzie had started smoking for the first time in her life; then again, everybody in Italy seemed to smoke). Now and again she would glance at the headlines of the *International Herald Tribune,* the English-speaking newspaper, though as her Italian got better, she found herself ignoring the *Tribune* and instead scanning *La Repubblica* and *Il Messaggero,* two of the more popular Italian dailies. After recess, there were more drawing classes, followed by lunch at one of the neighborhood trattorias. The afternoons were devoted to demonstrations of various conservation tech-niques—cleaning, repainting, retouching, and panel work—but students were not permitted to do any real hands-on work themselves until the second or the third year.

Despite her grueling class schedule, and the part-time job she'd found as a researcher at the American consulate in order to pay her bills, Lizzie was occasionally homesick, par-ticularly around the holidays. Without a telephone, she'd taken to writing her parents long letters every week, and the first time she reached them from a pay phone only to learn that none of her letters had arrived, Lizzie burst into tears. "I don't even bother sending letters in this country anymore," Donatella told her afterward in consolation. "The Italian postal service is famous for being a mess." When the phone company finally got around to installing a phone in her apartment—helped along by a small bribe from Donatella—Lizzie was overjoyed. From then on she made it a point to call home every week, though she was always surprised when her parents called her Lizzie, since by then the whole world, it seemed, including her *professori,* had taken to calling her by her Italian nickname of Betta.

Lizzie's first summer back home in Wisconsin came as a shock. Life in the Midwest seemed suddenly flat and somehow graceless, like a monotonous voice, and her old job at the real-estate office felt tedious and depressing. Many of her old friends from high school were already making plans to marry, and few if any of them seemed interested in leaving Argyle, much less the state—certainly not the country. Her parents were getting older, Lizzie noticed, and this pained her as well. Her father moved more slowly than she remembered, and retiring to his bedroom at night, he would pause for breath halfway up the back stairwell. "Just taking time to smell the roses," he said whenever he caught her staring at him in a concerned way.

One day, Lizzie informed her parents that she was going to prepare dinner for them that Friday night. "I don't want either of you to lift a finger," she announced, and proceeded to spend the better part of two afternoons in a row in a frustrating but ultimately successful search for fresh rosemary and sage, and porcini mushrooms. On Friday night, when she finally brought the pasta dish to the table with great fanfare, she was surprised by her parents' muted reaction. "This is great, Liz," her father kept saying, but Lizzie noticed her mother's silence, and later that night she went into her parents' bedroom, where her mother was buttoning up her nightgown. "Was dinner really terrible?" she asked almost timidly from the doorway.

"It was delicious," her mother replied. She was silent. "My feelings are hurt, that's all. I guess to me, it felt like you were saying that my cooking is boring, and not very good, and here you fly in from Rome—"

"Oh, Mom, I'm so sorry. I just thought it would be fun—"

"It *was* fun," she said. "It was so much fun. I guess it's just that my life seems a little dull all of a sudden, compared to yours." Her voice was suddenly intense. "This is why you have to have love, and your family, but you also have to have something *else*." She gazed up at Lizzie, her eyes moist. "I'm sorry. This isn't fair to you. I loved what you cooked, honey."

It saddened Lizzie a little how happy and relieved she was to return to Rome in preparation for her second year at the Istituto. She was overjoyed again to hear the sound of the bells in the morning and in the evening, the hundreds of church domes dotting the city like caps, and the beautiful, solitary cypress trees. She loved seeing Romans again, the dark beauty of the men, and the sophistication and vitality of the women, as well as the exquisitely dressed Roman children she saw in strollers, in the city parks, and romping around the obelisk at the Piazza del Popolo. Most of all, she loved seeing the art again—the exquisite sculptures, the frescoes, the panel paintings—noticing, not for the first time, how casually and unselfconsciously art and the past combined with everyday Roman life.

"I am in Rome, Italy," Lizzie kept reminding herself happily, and at those moments Argyle, Wisconsin, seemed as distant as a faraway planet. Even juggling her job at the American consulate and resuming classes at the Istituto seemed manageable. *Dear Dad*, Lizzie wrote home a few weeks later. *They are teaching me how to retouch watercolors and drawings! I am not all that good at it yet, but in a few months— or maybe next year—they'll let me start working on actual oil paintings, that is if I don't screw up too terribly before then.*

By far, Lizzie's favorite part of the city was the Piazza Navona, located just a few short blocks away from the Pantheon. In the late afternoon, after classes, she liked to take her sketch pad and her charcoal, or sometimes a watercolor kit and several of her favorite brushes, and sketch the side of a particular building, or a church, or even the grillwork of a restaurant. She was particularly taken by Bernini's Fontana dei Fiumi, an enormous flowing fountain in the center of the piazza, in which four great rivers—the Ganges, the Danube, the Nile, and the Plata—were represented by four

towering stone giants. At dusk every evening, when the piazza started filling up with people, mostly young foreigners,
talking, laughing, gesturing, trailing clouds of cigarette
smoke and perfume, Lizzie felt most acutely that she was
abroad, in this strange, beautiful, mysterious country called
Italy.

Now and again she felt tempted to run up to the nearest
American, and start chattering away in English about something, anything at all. But at the same time Lizzie secretly
wanted the American tourists she saw to perceive her as a
native, just another aspiring Roman artist passing the early
evening in the piazza, as so many other Italian women her
age did.

One night early in December, Lizzie was seated in her
favorite spot, sketching the Fontana dei Fiumi. The light
that evening in the Piazza Navona was spectacular, and the
buildings on either side of her radiated a glazed, lemon-
colored light. Christmas was approaching, the smell of roast-
ing chestnuts filled the air, and the Piazza Navona was
covered with raised tents, some filled with *presepi*—manger
scenes—others crowded with figures of the Befana, or the
Christmas witch, the Italian version of Santa Claus, who
rode around on a broomstick delivering presents to good
children and *carbone*—sugar coal—to the children who had
misbehaved.

Hearing the shout of English spoken from the other side
of the piazza, Lizzie was all of a sudden overcome by acute
homesickness. Putting aside her sketch pad, she took out the

photos of her family from her wallet. There was her mother, sitting on the back steps of her family's house, squinting and smiling; and there was her father in his favorite red leather armchair, his eyebrows slightly cocked, a familiar weariness in his eyes. Lizzie pictured the big tree in the living room, Frank Sinatra and Nat King Cole singing Christmas carols in the background, the smells of homemade pies wafting in from the kitchen, her brothers and sisters laughing and talking. She had wanted to go home for Christmas, but the plane fare was too steep. Now, with Donatella away in Milan with her boyfriend for the holidays, Lizzie was alone for Christmas for the first time ever in her life.

The lovely light was disappearing. Lizzie stuffed the photos back in her wallet, zipped up her purse, and resumed sketching one of the great stone giants in the Fontana dei Fiumi.

She was finishing up the beard when she looked up and noticed a group of young children standing less than six feet away from her, observing her intently. The children—and there must have been half a dozen of them—did not look Italian, but were instead swarthy looking and dressed in ragged clothing.

Excited by the thought that the children were interested in what she was drawing, Lizzie smiled and tilted her pad to reveal her sketch. As she did, one of the them, a beautiful, dusky-faced boy with a snub nose and fiercely glittering eyes, grabbed her pad with surprising roughness, peered at it, then uttered something curt in a language that wasn't

Italian. For the first time since she arrived in Rome, Lizzie could feel the beginnings of fear in her stomach. Snapping her pad shut, she stood up to go, but to her shock, she found herself blocked by the children, who had formed a gradually tightening ring around her. Before she knew it, their quick fingers were all over her body and around her purse.

"Va te ne!" Lizzie shouted. *"Vada via! Lasciami!"* Was this the right thing to say? Or had she said something wrong again? But by then, as quickly as they had come, the children scattered into the crowd. Trembling, she stood there for a moment, her heart pounding. It was when she glanced down to see if her handbag was still there that she noticed the huge curved tear in the leather, like a horrible grin. She didn't even bother to check inside her purse. She knew that her wallet—her money, her checkbook, the credit card her father had given her for emergencies, and most important, the photographs of her family—was gone forever.

Almost in a trance, Lizzie began making her way across the Piazza di Pasquino. She was almost at the corner of the Corso Vittorio Emanuele, when she felt a light tapping on her shoulder. Startled, and anticipating the worst, she turned to see one of the children who just ten minutes earlier had robbed her of her wallet.

"Lasciami!" Lizzie yelled again. She was about to make a run for it when the child, a pretty little girl dressed in an old smock and ragged sandals, dropped something at her feet, before dashing off into the nighttime Roman crowds.

A moment later Lizzie glanced down in amazement. It was the photographs of her family—her mother, her father, her brothers and sisters.

Lizzie didn't know whether to laugh or cry. Thieves with a heart, was all she could think to herself. Overcome by this strangely touching gesture, and aware that tears were beginning to prick her eyes, she waited for the cars to subside so she could cross the Corso Vittorio Emanuele. But there was a lot of nighttime traffic, the little *quattrocentos* and motor scooters racing around the corners, barely stopping to acknowledge the red lights, and every time she took a few steps off the curb and into the street, another car or Vespa came zooming toward her, forcing her back onto the sidewalk.

Lizzie wasn't quite sure why her tears came in earnest then. Why she found herself leaning up against a bank building on the Corso Vittorio Emanuele, covering her eyes and her mouth with her hands until her shoulders were shaking. Despite her mastery of certain details of Italian life—bus passes, stamps, food shopping, dry cleaning, and all the Italian she'd learned so far—she felt suddenly she was no match for Rome, no match for this sprawling, chattering, antiquity-filled city. With a single incident, a single unrehearsed strike, Rome had revealed her as a small-town Midwestern American girl who wasn't even capable of crossing the street.

She didn't even notice the young man who had appeared beside her, and who was glancing at her quizzically, up and down. *"Signorina, ch'é successo?"* he asked her softly. "Are you all right?"

Lizzie's first impulse was to run, since for all she knew, he might be another thief. But when she glanced up through her tears, she saw what she saw: a handsome Italian young man holding out a handkerchief. After a moment's hesitation Lizzie took it. *"Parla inglese?"* she asked through her tears.

The young man grimaced humorously. "Yah, I speak a little bit."

Fighting back her tears, Lizzie told him what had just happened. "A bunch of children!" she exclaimed. "And now I'm trying to get back to my apartment, and I—I—"

"Take my arm," the young man ordered, his voice surprisingly harsh, and although Lizzie was at first hesitant, she did as he said. A moment later the young man was escorting her purposefully across the Corso Vittorio Emanuele, glaring at the cars and the scooters that slowed for his crossing, revving up again the moment they were beyond them. When they reached the other side, the young man reluctantly released her arm.

"Mi dispiace," Lizzie said. "I'm sorry." These were still the Italian words she knew best. Then, still in Italian; "You must think I'm pathetic."

"No, no, don't be ridiculous." The young man was speaking Italian now, but patiently, for Lizzie's benefit. "In Rome, the rule of traffic is kill or be killed. A thousand years ago chariots drove these streets, with blades in front of them, and nothing has changed since that time. It sounds like you have been having a terrible day. You said you were robbed, what did they take from you, you are American, right?"

When Lizzie explained what had happened, the young man shook his head. *"Zingari,"* he said disgustedly, adding that gypsy children in Italy were known for distracting unsuspecting tourists, then taking off with their wallet or their wristwatch. "They cut women's purses with a knife, or scissors, take their wallets, they hide them under their armpits. That's so if they are caught—of course they never are, because they are fast as the wind—they can lift up their shirts to show there is nothing hidden in their pants or their skirts. *Cretini,"* he went on before bowing at her shyly. "I apologize on behalf of my city, signorina. As a Roman, I am ashamed that this happened to you."

"It's not your fault," Lizzie said with a little laugh. Already, to her surprise, she was feeling much better.

"It *is* my fault, because I am a Roman. But please give me and my city another chance!"

"Do you think I should go to the police?" Lizzie asked.

The young man twisted his lips in derision. *"I carabinieri sono incapaci, non fano un tubo,"* he replied, before breaking into English. "The gypsies in Rome are exceptionally well organized. Plus, the basis of Italy is not the law, it is the family. Why?" The young man laughed. "Because there is no law! Oh, well, the food is good and the climate is excellent."

For the first time Lizzie was able to take a good look at

this young man who had come to her rescue. He was tall and lean—had she ever seen anybody so lean?—with a proudly handsome face, dark brown eyes, and full lips. When he looked back at her unselfconsciously—and with evident appreciation—she had the curious impression that nobody had ever examined her face before in quite so thorough a way as he was doing. It was as though he were looking through her, seeing things inside her that she was unable to see in herself. A moment later the young man rose, and grasping Lizzie's hand and shaking it once, up and down, before releasing it again, he introduced himself as Masimilliano Caracci. Then: "What is your name?"

"Lizzie Orman," she replied.

Masimilliano Caracci leaned in to her. "Li, I am offended by the idea of Rome taking advantage of someone like you."

Momentarily, Lizzie found herself charmed by the nickname—"Li." "It's my own dumb fault," she said. "If I weren't such a wimp."

"Wimp? What is wimp? I don't know wimp. Is wimp like an umbrella? No, wait, it is what Zorro uses—" He mimed lashing the air with a whip, and Lizzie burst out laughing.

"A wimp is a scared person. With glasses," she explained, though she knew she looked nothing at all like a wimp, and for that matter, never had. Her dark blond hair hung halfway down to her shoulders, she had the blond, open looks of the Midwest, and in fact, most men considered her beautiful.

Masi stared at her. "You may think I am being rude," he said, "but I would like to hold your arm and lead you across many more streets during your stay here in Rome. So when will I get to see you again?"

Later Lizzie would think back on this dark Roman evening when the two of them first met. She would remember the darkening purple sky, the buzz of the motor scooters, the smell of oil cooking from a nearby apartment.

If she had felt a little more in control of herself, she told herself afterward, if on that particular day Rome hadn't conspired to frighten her, and to make her feel so alone and so homesick, she might have thanked Masimilliano Caracci politely, and returned to her apartment. Why trust a stranger, after all? Especially if you were a foreigner in a strange country, and you didn't know the language that well? But Lizzie knew that even if she had had all the self-possession in the world at that moment, she would have told Masi where she lived, and that she was a student at the Istituto del Restauro—when she told him that, Masi's eyes grew wide and excited. "You love art, the same way I do! Me, I attend the Giuliocesare! This is like *fate* practically!"—and that no, she knew practically nobody in Rome, and that *si*, she would be happy to have dinner with him that Friday evening. Then, wildly, feeling as though things were moving too fast, she added, "But I don't even know you, Masi!"

Masi—earlier, he had told Lizzie that no one called him "Masimilliano" but his mother—looked a little annoyed and surprised by her answer. "Well, here I am giving you the opportunity to know me! How could you pass that up?" He stared at her. "Scooter or your two feet?"

"I'm sorry, what?"

"Scooter or your two feet? Do I take you back home on my scooter, or do we walk?"

Masi escorted her back to the Via dei Pettinari, and though Lizzie had felt a little nervous about showing him where she lived, her anxiety quickly vanished as the two of them made their way through the side streets of Rome. "You must be crazy if you really think I'd ever get on one of those scooters," she remarked at one point, but Masi simply grimaced. "Like everything in life, you must try it first before you say no," he said. Several times, when Lizzie caught sight of Masi's profile, she was struck by how much he looked like a character from a turn-of-the-century painting, though she kept this thought to herself. "So what is the Giuliocesare?" she asked at one point.

Masi explained that the the Giuliocesare was a *liceo classico*, a local university, that he was in his final year there, and that like most state colleges, it was free to Italians. "Say what you like about Italy, Li," he added. "They take care of us."

"Do you live in a dormitory?" Lizzie asked.

Masi seemed surprised at the question. "I live with my family, of course."

By now they had arrived in front of her apartment. "I can't thank you enough," Lizzie said in Italian. "Really."

Masi's mouth crinkled into a smile. *"Dilo di nuovo,"* he said. "Say that again." When Lizzie repeated what she'd said, he smiled at her for a second time. "I love that," he said.

"You love what? What did I just say wrong?"

"I like hearing you make a little mistake in Italian, that's all. Don't be offended, please," Masi added. "I forgot sometimes that when you speak Italian, or I speak English, there is so much that we cannot say, really. When you speak to me in Italian, it is in translation. When I speak to you in English, it is in translation." There was a faint sadness in his eyes. "Maybe someday we will reach a time when there is no translation, when it's just"—he made a zipping sound with his lips—"like that."

"So I'll see you Friday, okay?" Lizzie said, embarrassed suddenly.

"Friday." Masi put out his hand again in that comical fashion that Lizzie had noticed many Europeans did when shaking hands, grasping her hand once, up and down, then releasing it, before darting off down the street.

That week at the Istituto del Restauro, the professors were training the students how to copy works of art in different scales, a process that involved grids and rulers. It was exacting work, and if a student lost concentration for one moment, he or she could make a crucial mistake. Yet despite this time-intensive work, Lizzie could not get Masi out of her mind, and she found herself counting the days impatiently until the end of the week. But that Friday afternoon, when she handed in her assignment to her *professore,* he scanned it, then immediately handed it back to her. "Try again, until you get it right," he said sternly. For the next four hours, long after the other students had dispersed into the Roman dusk, Lizzie copied and recopied the triangular portion of the Tintoretto painting until she and her professor were satisfied, and by the time she reached her apartment building, where Masi was waiting outside, he looked annoyed. "So your work is more important than me?" he demanded sourly. "Have you met somebody else? Another guy?"

Thinking he was joking, Lizzie didn't reply, but when he asked again, she realized that he meant it. "I don't know that many men in Rome, actually," she replied, "except for you." She felt vaguely flattered when Masi seemed satisfied and relieved by her answer.

"Do you remember the scooter-versus-the-two-feet conversation you and I had when I met you?"

Lizzie nodded.

"Well, I say we have done the two feet already, so now it is time for the scooter." Masi escorted her over to a small, gleaming, black Vespa, and told her to climb on behind him.

"You're not going to make me ride on that thing are you?" she asked, but Masi looked impatient. "Just hold on to my back. I am a very safe driver. Fast but safe," he added.

The restaurant was less than a mile away, in the old Jewish Quarter, and Lizzie hung on for dear life as Masi raced and whipped through the rain-soaked *vicoli,* the narrow, winding side streets. Despite her fear, it felt good, holding this young man around the waist, feeling the beat of his heart and the sharpness of his rib cage. Ten minutes later Masi pulled up in front of a small trattoria.

"It's a little early, isn't it?" Lizzie asked, getting off the scooter and trying to get her balance back. Since she had arrived in Rome, she often found herself hungry at all the wrong times, since dinner in Italy typically didn't begin until at least eight. The sign on the restaurant door said CHIUSO—closed—but Masi pounded on the glass. Eventually, a middle-aged man came to the door, and seeming to recognize Masi, opened it wide. "I knew that as an American you would probably be starving by now," Masi said to Lizzie, "so I arranged with my friend here for us to eat a little early."

It was quite possibly the best dinner Lizzie had ever eaten in her life: *ribollita,* a thick Tuscan bean soup, followed by *carciofi alla Giudea,* fried artichoke hearts, followed by a delicate pumpkin squash risotto, and for dessert, *palle de nonno,* consisting of cream puffs filled with sweet ricotta, mixed in with shards of chocolate.

"What's *palle de nonno* mean?" Lizzie asked, and Masi looked at her gravely.

"I'm afraid, *tesoro,* that it means 'grandfather's balls.' "

Lulled by the bottle of red table wine, Lizzie found herself eager to tell Masi everything she could about herself—her ambitions to be a painter, her brothers and sisters, her family back at home in the Midwest. She couldn't help thinking about the other men she'd been involved with in her life: the boys from high school and college. *Boys:* she couldn't help but think of them now as boys, jumpy and mercurial and eager to get her into bed, torn between their attraction to her and their feeling that falling in love somehow made them less male, boys who seemed to find conversation a waste of time, and who seemed to want to get their formal educations over with as soon as possible so they would never have to think, or be challenged, or risk having an opinion again. Boys who considered talking a stumbling block to love and romance, rather than a part of getting to know and appreciate another person.

Lizzie knew this much: never before had she been around a young man, Masi, who listened to her so intently, who seemed to be observing her so carefully, who noticed when her wineglass was empty, or how emotional it made her to talk about life back home. At one point he brushed a crumb from her lip, and the sensation of his finger against her cheek made her stomach feel weak. When he insisted on feeding her a forkful of his dinner and later on, his dessert, she could only stare back at him, amazed. American men were afraid of women, Lizzie realized at one point, and the frank, unembarrassed intensity of Masi's gaze came as both a surprise and a revelation. Two hours later she thought to herself, I am under this man's spell.

Lizzie found out more about Masi, too. He had grown up in Rome, *"borghese, non ricco, ma anche non povero"* (not rich, but not poor either), raised mostly by his mother, since his father worked long hours at a factory. Masi spoke adoringly of his mother—"My mother, she is an amazing woman. Tiny. But strong"—but when the subject turned to his father, he hesitated, and then looked angry. "He is not all that good to my mother. Other women, you know?" He shrugged. "Still, he works hard for us, he is a good man."

Lizzie had never met anybody quite so cultured, anybody who could talk about so many subjects: opera, politics, finance, theater, science, literature, history, and of course, art and artists. Though the university that Masi attended cost him nothing, he worked after school in an art gallery on the Via Margutta that specialized in modern art, which he hated. "People call themselves artists, they just throw pigment against the canvas, some of it sticks, and they call it art," he said disgustedly. "Someday I am going to be an art dealer. I don't have talent myself as an artist, but I have always had an eye for what is good and what is not good. I learn. What people don't teach me, I teach myself. What do you call this in English? 'Self-taught.'" Masi shrugged. "If my ambition works out, it works out. If it doesn't, it doesn't." He laughed. "Nobody on their deathbed sits around saying over and over again, 'Oh, my goodness, I should have worked harder during my life!' There is so much I want to do before I settle down and have a job." His dark eyes burned into Lizzie's. "You know?"

Despite her protests, Masi insisted on picking up the check. "I want to see you again and again and again," he told Lizzie as he dropped her off in front of her apartment that night. He added, in halting English, "I want to keep you in my pocket all day, Li. So you and I will never be apart."

Lizzie gazed back at him. She had never felt this way about a man before, not in her whole life, and it felt dangerous, as though she were teetering on the edge of something, and the sheer drop, if she dared to look down, might well devastate her. She loved everything about Masi: the way he spoke, the way he looked, the way he moved, the way he looked at life. She had never thought it was possible to feel so strongly about another person.

"I want to be with you, too, Masi," Lizzie said simply. And then she turned and went into her building.

For the next few months the two of them were practically inseparable. Like most Italians, Masi was proud of his city, and he made it a point to show Lizzie a side of Rome that few foreigners ever got to see. On their first excursion, she had come armed with a map, but he placed it on top of a garbage can. "Maps are for dopes and tourists," he said. "Rome believes in keeping most of its secrets hidden from sight. Think of oysters that hide their pearls. Italy is just like that."

Instead of taking Lizzie to obvious tourist sites, many of which she'd already visited, Masi took her to small out-of-the-way places, like the Church of Sant'Agostino, where he led her into a back chamber. "This church is the oyster," he said, "and up there"—he pointed to the Caravaggio painting hanging dramatically on the far wall—"is your pearl." On the Aventine, in the Piazza dei Cavalieri di Malta, Masi showed her a tiny keyhole in a wall that offered an expansive view of St. Peter's Cathedral. One rainy afternoon, he took her to the Via Margutta and showed her the gallery where he worked. "This is the street where I will have a gallery someday," he said to Lizzie. "I will be an old, happy Italian man, driving a Lancia, or an Alfa-Romeo. And I will be allowed to spend the afternoon in the Vatican Gardens whenever I wish."

The Vatican Gardens, Masi explained, were closed off to the public, and only the pope, and the pope's inner circle, as well as various local dignitaries, were allowed to enter them. "They say they are the most beautiful gardens in all of Rome." His voice was fierce. "I will get there someday, you will see. Come," he added, taking her hand tightly and leading her in the direction of a small open-air fruit market. "I'll bet you have never in your life tasted a blood orange."

It wasn't just the sights of Rome that Masi was eager to introduce Lizzie to, it was food. Though Donatella had introduced her early on to Sambuca and *tiramisù* (not to mention baby octopuses, which Lizzie found to her shock she actually liked), Masi relished his country's cuisine and took a special delight in preparing meals for Lizzie. Two weeks after their first meeting, when Donatella was again away for the weekend visiting her boyfriend in Milan, Masi invited himself over to Lizzie's apartment, and as Lizzie looked on, he plunged several bunches of broccoli rabe into boiling water. Atop a separate burner he began frying up tiny bits of garlic in hot olive oil, eventually removing the tiny browned triangles and setting them aside. "For flavoring only," he explained.

Lizzie watched, fascinated, as Masi dropped anchovies into the sizzling olive oil until they had dissolved, adding a few red hot pepper flakes to the mix. When the broccoli rabe was done cooking, he drained it in a colander, adding a bag of fresh *orecchiette* pasta to the boiling water. When the pasta was al dente, Masi mixed everything together, and served it in a steaming bowl. When Lizzie asked whether Masi had any Parmesan cheese, he shuddered. "Li, *never*, ever with this kind of pasta!" he said emphatically.

Afterward, they sat together on the old, hard-backed couch that Donatella had found at a local flea market, and when Masi moved closer and put his arm around Lizzie's shoulder, she yielded to his chest and arms. A moment later his mouth was on hers, and she responded, pulling back a few minutes later for air. "Your lips are like pillows," she remarked with a small laugh. Masi was breathing heavily. "I cannot help what my lips feel like," he said seriously, and despite herself, Lizzie laughed. "I actually love pillows," she said, kissing him again, this time not pulling away.

Minutes later, no longer able to contain themselves, they made their way over to Lizzie's small bedroom. Masi's body was hard and smooth, and it fit perfectly with Lizzie's own.

Gazing at his face above hers, she hugged him close to her, until she was warm again, then hot, then finally, breathlessly, cool again as the October night coming in through the window caused her to snuggle next to Masi, who lay naked beside her, his chest gently rising and falling. A moment later he walked proudly naked across the room, his body slightly damp with sweat. In America, Lizzie might have been slightly startled by the display of the naked male form, but living in Rome, where unclothed statues of both men and women filled the piazzas and the museums, she had long grown accustomed to the beauty of both sexes.

Still later the two of them lay in the dim glow of the bedroom, Masi clinging sleepily to her back. "Here is where you and I need no translation to talk to each other," he murmured. "Right?"

"Right," Lizzie replied sleepily.

He turned to her suddenly. "Li?" he said, in the same sleepy voice.

"Yes?"

Masi's English was careful and tentative, as though he had been practicing. "I love thee."

Lizzie couldn't help but let out a small giggle. "Now where in the world did you ever learn that word *thee*?"

"It's not the right word?" Masi seemed offended. He'd been practicing his English, he said, by reading parts of the King James Bible a friend had found for him in an English-language bookstore.

"No," Lizzie said, "it is the right word." She was silent. "I love thee, too." She added, "I hope someday maybe you and I can walk in the Vatican Gardens together."

Masi took her in his arms. "It will happen. We will be married, you see, and you will be the mother of our beautiful children."

"What shall we name them?" she asked, enjoying this game.

"Hmm." Masi pondered this, stroking his chin. "I say that if we have a boy, we name him Flavio. Or Ulysse."

"Ulysse?" Lizzie exclaimed with a laugh. "You mean, like Ulysses?"

Masi laughed, too. "Yes. He will grow up to be a great explorer."

"I don't like either of those names very much, Masi."

"What do you want, you want to call him 'Jeff' or 'Bob' or 'Danny'?" His flat American accent made Lizzie laugh. "And for a little girl," Masi went on, "I have always loved the name of Patrizia."

"I love the name Patrizia, too," Lizzie murmured. Then: "Do you think I'm ever going to get to see where you live?"

In the dark, she could sense Masi's grimace. "Yes, yes, of course," came his softly impatient answer. "One of these days."

With the floodgates finally opened, it seemed that over the next few weeks all Lizzie and Masi did was make love— though always at her apartment, in the small bed with its triangular view of gray sky during the day, and its triangle of stars at night. By now, Donatella was spending practically every weekend with her boyfriend in Milan, so Lizzie and Masi usually had the apartment on the Via dei Pettinari to themselves.

Lizzie had had several boyfriends in high school and in college, but she had never felt so ravenous about a young man before, or so full of desire. And she had learned to cope with Masi's jealousy. "Where did you learn how to do that?" he asked her once, softly, after a particularly passionate encounter. The question took her by surprise. "I just . . . did it. For you. You inspired me, I guess." When he didn't reply, she pressed him. "What's wrong?"

For a long time he didn't answer. At last he said, "I cannot bear the idea of you doing the same things that we do with another man," and though Lizzie snuggled up next to him, and told him that she never *wanted* to make love to anybody else, Masi didn't shake out of his dark mood until the next morning.

One Friday afternoon, Masi turned to Lizzie as he was walking her back home from his classes at the Giuliocesare. "Tonight," he said, bowing at her formally, "you will do me the honor of coming to dinner at my house."

Early on, Donatella had warned Lizzie about Italian men and their families. "This country is not really based on machismo," she'd said once "It's based on what we call *mammismo*."

"What's *mammismo*?" Lizzie asked, and Donatella had looked at her with humor and pity. "Unfortunately, it's just what it sounds like. The mama is king in Italy. She is both mother and father. The son does not dare cross her."

Early that Friday evening, Donatella helped her choose what she was going to wear, though Lizzie was shocked when Donatella picked out her least attractive dress and laid it across the bed. "This is perfect," said Donatella, laughing. "Trust me, you don't want to look too pretty."

"Why?" But Donatella only laughed.

Masi picked her up on his Vespa, and they took a long trip to Fiumicino, on the outskirts of Rome, near the airport. It was poorer, here, obviously, with rickety stoops, and pale unwashed buildings, and lines of drying laundry hanging overhead. As they ascended the four floors of the apartment building, Masi seemed distracted, and before ringing the bell, he touched Lizzie's shoulder briefly, warmly. It was the very last time he touched her that evening.

Overly concerned about making a good impression, Lizzie later found that the details of that night blurred into one: Masi's small, imperious mother with her surprisingly strong handshake, Masi's father, equally small but beaten down, saying barely a single word but instead gazing, before and even during dinner, at the small flickering black-and-white television in a corner of the dining room, the simple, delicious food. All the details blurred in her mind except for one: Masi introducing her to his family as a American student studying in Rome, then barely glancing at her during the rest of the evening. An American student. Not his girlfriend, not his lover, not even his friend. Afterward, on the street outside Masi's apartment building, Lizzie, incensed, told him that she was walking back home. "Are you angry at me?" he called after her. "What for?"

Lizzie whirled around. "What for? I'm just some American student that you met? Some visitor? Is that all I am to you?"

"You don't understand," Masi replied. He spoke in English, for Lizzie's benefit. "One has to be so careful. This country, it is much more formal—"

Lizzie didn't let him finish. "Are you embarrassed by me, is that it?"

When Masi seized both her arms, at first Lizzie tried to pull away. "Listen to me," he said loudly. "You are the only woman I have ever loved in my life. *Ever.* I want to spend all my time with you. All my days, all my nights." He paused. "In a month's time it will be the summer again. I will not have classes, and you will not have classes. I have some money saved up from my job, not much but a little. Will you come traveling with me in Italy, and let me show you my country?"

Although her parents expected her to spend the summer in Wisconsin—Lizzie had received several postcards from them, telling her that her old room was waiting, and that her father was ready to pay for her airfare home—she suddenly could not bear the idea of another claustrophobic Midwestern summer, and another three months working at the real-estate office, chattering with the other women over coffee and doughnuts. Picturing her old bedroom, she realized with great sorrow that it no longer fit the woman that she had become. Plus, the idea of not seeing Masi for three months was more than she could bear.

"I will go anywhere with you," she said to him.

Masi had managed to borrow a car from his older brother, an ancient, lime-green Fiat, and together the two of them left Rome on a warm summer afternoon in June, taking a brief detour south to attend the wine festival in Marino, in the Castelli Romani, where they stood delightedly watching the red wine flowing freely from the fountain in the piazza. From Marino, they traveled north, to Todi, and then to Siena. To her surprise, Masi knew as much about other cities and towns as he knew about Rome. "Remember, we have only been a united country for one hundred and sixty years," he informed her once, shrugging. "There is still a great division between the north and the south of Italy, just like in your country."

"People need to have enemies. I think it's human nature," Lizzie remarked in Italian. By now, her grasp of the language was good enough that she and Masi spoke almost exclusively in Italian. Recently, she had even begun to dream in Italian; and she had noticed that she was taking many more pains with her appearance than when she'd first arrived in Italy. During her first few months in Rome she'd been fascinated, and also perplexed, by how much attention Donatella gave to her appearance, how she would dress up in a tight, fashionable skirt and high heels even if she was merely popping outside to pick up a pastry, or going to the *tabaccaio* for a pack of stamps. When Lizzie remarked on it, Donatella explained that in Italy, people were often judged, fairly or not, on how they looked.

"For example," she told her once, "people who have never visited Italy think all Italians must be so overweight because we love our food, but you tell me, have you seen one overweight Italian person since you came here?" Lizzie had to admit that she hadn't. "It is the same with clothing," Donatella said. "For all the *La Dolce Vita* stuff you hear about in America, we are a very formal, structured country. The men have their uniforms, and so do the women." Following this conversation, Lizzie had made a concerted effort to look her best at all times, and she knew how much this pleased Masi. I'm becoming old-fashioned, she thought to herself, and the strange part is I like it, too.

It hadn't been easy for Lizzie to tell her parents she wouldn't be coming home to Wisconsin that summer. "So what's the guy's name?" her father asked her almost immediately. "Dad—" Lizzie said after a moment. Then: "Okay, it's Masi." "And is he good to you?" her father asked. "Yes," she said. "Very." "If he's not good to you, will you tell me?" "Yes, Daddy, I will." Lizzie's father was silent. "Please be careful, honey," he said. Three days later she received an envelope her father had sent care of the nearest American Express office, containing a check for five hundred dollars, as well as a brief letter:

Dear Lizzie,

*It is no fun being in a foreign country with no money. I
found this out during the war in Korea! I hope this helps
with your summer. We miss you, but we understand.*

Love Daddy.

*P.S. Please give my regards to your friend Masi. If you
love him, I am sure he must be wonderful. P.P.S. He
better be.*

At the beginning of their trip, Masi and Lizzie pooled
their resources, allotting themselves a certain fixed amount
to spend every day, including on gasoline for the car, though
Masi insisted on being in charge of their itinerary. Nights
they spent on the floors of inexpensive hostels, or with college friends of Masi's, though they left his second cousin's
house in Todi earlier than planned because, according to
Masi, "I didn't like the way he was staring at you."

"I was just talking to him," Lizzie said, exasperated, si-
multaneously flattered and annoyed by Masi's jealousy. Still,
distracted by the glorious scenery of the countryside, she
soon forgot their differences. In Florence, they ate a picnic
lunch in the Boboli Gardens, and spent a long weekend
wandering through the city's museums and piazzas. As they
stood marveling at the sculpture of David, Masi murmured,
"You know that Michelangelo was convinced that the figures that he sculpted were already in the rock, waiting for

him to come along with his chisel, to give them life?" About Renoir, he said, "You know Renoir hated the word *flesh*. He thought that it was too much like 'meat.' He preferred telling critics that he painted 'skin.' And he did that, painted skin, better than almost anybody else." At the end of the day, when she complained of dizziness and exhaustion, he actually looked pleased. "You have Stendhal's syndrome!" he cried, explaining that Stendhal's syndrome was a well-known ailment marked by seeing too much art too quickly. "We will go back to the hostel, and there I will wait on you hand and foot."

Lizzie gazed at him. "I love thee, Masi," she said softly. It was their private exchange, a joke and at the same time truer than anything she had ever said, or felt, in her life.

"No, I love *thee,* Li."

Two days later they boarded a train to Venice, where Masi showed Lizzie the Ponte dei Sospiri—the Bridge of Sighs—and the old torture chambers underneath, and they drank Camparis at Harry's Bar, and Lizzie spent an entire afternoon sketching the pigeons in the Piazza San Marco. On their final day in Venice, she and Masi visited the magnificent Cathedral of Santa Maria Assunta, in Torcello, and on the way back stopped at the small islands of Murano and Burano, before taking a *vaporetto* to the Lido, where they wandered the sandy beaches in front of the huge hotel where Thomas Mann had written *Death in Venice*.

Back in Rome, Masi and Lizzie both resumed classes. And yet their separation during the day seemed only to make

Masi more and more attentive. Lizzie felt flattered by his attention, but also, at times, almost overwhelmed. Not once had he ever allowed her to buy food, or pay for a meal at a restaurant, and long ago she had learned never to discuss old boyfriends in front of him. Several times Masi had shown up unexpectedly at the Istituto when Lizzie's classes let out, once scowling darkly at the sight of her talking to a male classmate, and she'd had to spend the rest of the afternoon explaining that the classmate was nothing more than a friend. It seemed to her that Masi was attracted by her independence, but at the same time he wanted to suppress and control it.

"What can I say?" Donatella told Lizzie once. "He's a typical Italian male. There are advantages, and disadvantages."

Still, as classes got under way at the Istituto, Lizzie put most of these thoughts aside. By now she felt like an old hand at art conservation. She'd been shocked the first time she'd seen the array of instruments that conservators used—the rows of scalpels, microscopes, and syringes always reminding her of a surgeon's office—but now these instruments felt as dear to her as old friends. During her first few months she was taught the basics of retouching, learning how to match colors and stay within the lines. Like most students, she started off with a watercolor palette before her *professori* allowed her to move on to oils. Now Lizzie was skilled enough that her instructors had started giving her hands-on work at the Palatine and the Forum, consolidating stone-coffered ceilings that were crumbling with age. Tapping the stones in an attempt to discover air pockets, and using a syringe, Lizzie injected Ladon, a milky adhesive, into the crumbling stones, then waited until they had hardened.

Masi was thrilled by her studies, and in between his own classes at the Giuliocesare, he took every possible opportunity to watch Lizzie at work. "Li, what you do is now a part of Rome," he announced one day. "A part of you will be here now forever and ever."

Lizzie simply shrugged. "It's not as hard as it looks, Masi. You don't have to be so melodramatic."

Six months later her *professori* gave her her first opportunity to clean an oil painting.

The painting she was given was done by a well-known Flemish artist named Giorno Hals. It was large, three feet by five feet, and it showed a pontiff draped in a red cloak sitting steadfastly on a chair in a garden. Her *professori* had warned her to clean only the sky, and the clouds behind the pope, that elsewhere the glazes were too vulnerable to be cleaned, and for the first several weeks Lizzie did as she was told, wetting the cotton tip with her tongue, and gently, diligently rubbing away at the accumulated dirt and age. (She still couldn't get over the fact that human saliva was one of the best ways to clean a painting, and yet her *professori* swore by it. "Excellent surface tension," one of them had told her with a twinkle in his eye. "Wonderful enzymatic qualities. Particularly good after a lunch when you have drunk plenty of red wine.")

One of the basic rules of art conservation was that a conservator should work as often as possible by natural light and Lizzie automatically opened up the shade to let in the light from the Via della Lagrima. As she made her way over to the easel, she found herself feeling strange, even dizzy, to the point that she had to steady herself against the table. It was hardly the first time she had felt this way in recent days; for the past couple of weeks she'd been feeling faint at certain times of the day, and for some reason, hungrier than usual, and no matter how much she ate, two hours later she was hungry again. Chalking up today's dizziness to skipping breakfast that morning, Lizzie set to work with her skewers and cotton. Every day for the next week she worked on the sky and the clouds, and every day she noticed an improvement. When she finished, she was positive that the sky and the clouds looked as they must have when Giorno Hals first painted them.

Lizzie completed her task two weeks later, much earlier than expected, and then a thought occurred suddenly to her. Why not clean the rest of the painting? Presumably, somebody else would be coming in anyway to perform the work—the pontiff, his red robe, his majestic chair—so why didn't she just save that person some time? And not to be arrogant, but hadn't she proved beyond doubt how adept she was at this?

Taking out another skewer, Lizzie attached a fresh piece of cotton to its tip, and began gently rubbing away at the pontiff's face. With every filthy piece of cotton, she was convinced that she was doing the right thing. Going through half a dozen cotton-tipped skewers, she delicately made inroads around the pontiff's nose and chin, rubbing away the soot that had accumulated around his mouth, and then she started on his eyes.

When the pontiff's left eyeball came off onto the cotton swab, Lizzie screamed.

Hearing the commotion, two *professori* came rushing into the room, glanced down at the painting, then glanced back up horrified at Lizzie, who was still holding up the stick with its pigment-smeared cotton tip, and immediately called out for a third *professore*. "*Mi dispiace, signori!*" Lizzie kept saying. "I was just trying to—"

She didn't finish, because she had no idea what she'd been trying to do. *Show off* were the first words that came to her mind. Prove that I know more than I actually do. She would never forget the words the *professori* used—*Idiota! Cretina! Ho detto che non dovevamo permetterla di lavorare su quel quadro!*—or how her favorite teacher, the one who had instructed her on how to clean paintings in the first place, glared at her and made a brisk whisking motion with his hands, as though he were a broom and Lizzie suddenly nothing more than a piece of dust.

Lizzie ran out of the building, in tears, not knowing where she was going. The faint, queasy feeling she'd had in her stomach for the past two weeks was intensifying, and the Roman heat, still brutal even though it was autumn, made her muscles feel weak, as though she were on the verge of falling. She had failed. She had blown her opportunity. She would be kicked out of the Istituto and sent back in shame to America, all because of her arrogance, her disobedience, her desire to show off that she could clean a painting better than anyone else in her class. She completely deserved her fate, whatever it was.

Only a few people saw Lizzie when she stumbled and fell onto the sidewalk—an elderly man smoking a pipe, a group of five or six teenage Italian boys, looking more American than most Americans, and various merchants closing up their shops for lunch. It was the teenagers who first alerted the *carabinieri,* and two hours later, when she awoke in a hospital bed, wearing a black blood-pressure cuff on her left arm, she had no idea where she was. A middle-aged nurse was sitting by her bedside, monitoring her blood pressure. "What happened to me?" Lizzie asked groggily in Italian.

Gently—and Lizzie would always remember, with great warmth—the nurse told her that she had fainted on the street and sustained a slight cut on her forehead, that her blood pressure had been dangerously low (though it was stabilized now), and the best news of all, if she hadn't known it already, was that Lizzie was *incinta*—pregnant. The nurse gazed at her, beaming. "Six or seven weeks. A summer baby." The nurse had delivered her own five children during the summer, too, she went on, and thank goodness she had been able to get away to the mountains on the weekends, because to be in your third trimester in Rome during the summer, well, you didn't even want to think about it. The nurse's joy and obvious excitement touched Lizzie, and cut like a knife through her incredulous shock. She'd had no idea she was pregnant, but suddenly it made sense: the dizziness she'd been feeling recently, the faintness, the fatigue, the unexpected appetite.

Lizzie asked for a telephone, and when the nurse brought one in, she dialed Masi's number at the Giuliocesare. A university secretary answered, and nearly ten minutes later she heard his breathless voice, saying, *"Pronto."* He sounded surprised and pleased to be hearing from her in the middle of the day, until she told him she was in the emergency room of the Gemelli Hospital.

"What happened?" Masi asked, his voice rising.

Lizzie hesitated. *"Sono incinta, Masi,"* she said finally, adding, "The nurse told me that the baby is due next summer."

For a long time Masi said nothing. Aware of the whimsical nature of the Italian national phone company, for a moment Lizzie worried that they had been disconnected. But then she heard his breathing again. "I'm shocked, Li," he said at last. "I don't know what to say, really."

"What about congratulations?" she suggested lightly, but Masi had already hung up the phone.

Lizzie found it hard to believe. A baby—Masi's baby, her baby. It was a fact, the two of them had often talked about kids, and about raising a family, and about Lizzie staying on in Rome once her classes ended, and not returning to the States. Now, lying in her hospital bed, it was hard not to fantasize about what their life would be like together: Masi running a successful art gallery, Lizzie taking a few years off to raise their child, then returning to art conservation part-time, trips back and forth to Italy and the United States, a little boy named Flavio, or Ulysse—well, maybe not Ulysse—or a little girl named Patrizia.

A moment later she realized that this was nothing more than an idiotic pipe dream. The reality would most likely be a cramped apartment (perhaps even moving in temporarily with Masi's family), two young, unprepared parents, an endless struggle for money. Perhaps she would not have the baby after all, or perhaps she would have the baby, then give him or her up for adoption. The thought momentarily doused her happiness.

But what did she want? Lizzie didn't know. Looking back over the past few years, it seemed suddenly to her as if she had journeyed from one point of vulnerability and indecision to the next. First, as a foreigner in a country where she hadn't been able to speak the language. Then as a student of conservation, an art, a craft, and a science all rolled into one, which she'd had to learn cold. Finally she had met a man whom she loved more than anyone she'd ever loved in her life, but who seemed determined to control most of her decisions. Where was she, Lizzie, in all of this?

Back at her apartment that night, she telephoned Masi again. "I am halfway out the door," he said to her, and she heard something in his voice that made her think he had been drinking, which struck her as strange; Masi rarely drank, and despite the availability of wine and liquor, drunkenness was frowned on in Italy. "I will call you later tonight, and we will talk." That evening, she waited by the phone, declining Donatella's invitation to join her for dinner with friends, but Masi never called, and the next morning his phone line was busy for four hours straight. Later that afternoon, Lizzie finally reached him at his parents' apartment. "I need to see you very badly," she said.

"I found out the name of an abortion doctor," Masi said in reply, his voice tight. "In Trastevere."

Momentarily, Lizzie was stunned. No, it did not make much sense to have a child right now, not as her studies at the Istituto were winding down, not as Masi was finishing up his final year at the Giuliocesare. But the fact that Masi had already made a decision on her behalf angered her. "Don't you think you and I should discuss this first?" she asked. To her surprise, her words came out automatically in English. It was as though she were reclaiming an identity she had cast aside since coming to Rome. "I'm pretty confused about the situation, Masi," she said, "and I really think we need to talk about it."

She could hear his fierce breathing on the other end of the phone. "I don't understand your English that well."

"You and I need to talk," she said, reverting to Italian.

"We are talking. Right now we are talking."

"I mean in person."

"Fine." Lizzie had never heard such brusqueness in Masi's voice. "Where?"

They made arrangements to meet that afternoon at the Piazza Navona at four-thirty. Lizzie showed up early and took a seat on the Fontana dei Fiumi, feeling agitated and slightly sick to her stomach. She felt an enormous swell of relief when she saw Masi coming toward her. They embraced, even though his arms felt strangely stiff and his manner seemed subdued, almost melancholy. For the first several minutes the two of them avoided the topic that had brought them both to the Piazza Navona, talking instead about foolish things— the spate of hot, overcast weather, Donatella's recent decision to move in with her boyfriend, who was studying medicine in Milan—but then Masi finally broke in, "So how did this thing—this pregnancy—happen, anyway?"

"I don't know," Lizzie said. "Maybe a space alien came down in the middle of the night." When he didn't laugh, she added, "How do *you* think it happened?"

"I don't know, you tell me. Have you been with other guys?"

Lizzie gazed back at him, shocked. "You're kidding me, right?"

"Were you?"

"I'm not even going to answer that question." When Masi frowned, she touched his cheek and was surprised when he flinched. "Of course, not, Masi. You're the only person I've been with."

"So were you being careful?"

"Yes." They had always been very careful to use protection. "But, Masi, I kind of resent your implying that this whole thing is my responsibility." Lizzie stopped suddenly. "Why are we arguing like this? Aren't you remotely happy about any of this?"

"You want me to lie, Li, then I will lie to you." Masi's features softened. "Of course, you know that I love you and I am happy to think that you are carrying my child. That is the part that makes me very happy."

"It does?" Lizzie had broken in at the first sign of his approval, and now, as his features hardened slightly, she felt foolish.

"But do I want you to have this child right now, at this moment in time, Li?" Masi went on. "No, I don't."

"Why?" she asked softly.

"Why?" He seemed to grow suddenly furious at the question. "Why? Why? A hundred thousand reasons why! Why can't you look the facts in the face? We are both twenty-two years old! That is too young! There is too much life ahead to be lived before I settle down to a bunch of screaming children! I want a career before I have a family! You can't actually be serious, can you?"

Masi came closer to Lizzie, and for the first time ever she felt scared of him. "I am a believer in the expression '*Il mundo è fatto a scale; c'e chi scende e c'e chi sale.*' " He translated in English, for Lizzie's benefit. "The world is made of stairs. There are those who go up, and those who go down." He almost spat out the last part. "To have a baby now would be to go *down* those stairs."

The expression on Lizzie's face must have signaled her hurt, and confusion, and now Masi shook his head violently. "No!" he shouted, and then again, "No!" By now, he was attracting the attention of the other people in the piazza, who were glancing over as though they were witnessing a theatrical performance. "I will not have a child hold my life hostage! I will not destroy my life because of some woman who will not look facts in the face, and who insists on having a baby when she is just a baby herself!"

"Masi, let's talk about it without getting hysterical," Lizzie said desperately. "You keep saying I'm destroying your life, but it's not just me who did this! And for God's sakes, stop trying to control my life every single second!"

"There is nothing more to talk about. I told you, I have the name of a doctor in Trastevere. He is discreet and not too expensive. I have made an appointment for you for next Thursday. You will not disobey me here!"

"Disobey you?" Lizzie repeated incredulously. "Who do you think you are, my father? You're treating me like a teenager!"

"That's because you're acting *stupid,* like a teenager."

Lizzie stood her ground. "So you are saying to me that if I have this baby—"

Masi interrupted harshly, enunciating every word, as if he were talking to a child. "*Questo ti dico molto chiaro: se decidi di continuare questa gravidanza, non voglio mai più vedere ni te ni il bambino.* Okay?"

For better or for worse, Lizzie had reached a point in her understanding of the Italian language, with its swoops and swerves, its slangy passion, that she understood precisely what Masi had just said.

"I am telling you that if you have this child, I will never see you or the child again. Do you understand this?"

Lizzie nodded. She understood perfectly. As Masi walked away, she wept.

By that Thursday morning, she had made up her mind, but first she had to return to the Istituto and face the consequences of destroying Giorno Hals's painting. She had just entered the lobby, on her way to a morning lecture at the auditorium, when one of her *professori,* the one who had made the shooing motion with his hands, spotted her and came over excitedly. *"Professore, mi dispiace——"* Lizzie started to say, but to her surprise, the professor was beaming. *"Ma che genio!"* he kept exclaiming. *"Mi pare incredibile che sapeva che cosa ci sia sotto l'occhio!"*

"I don't understand," Lizzie started to say, but she didn't finish. By then several other *professori* had surrounded her, each one chattering away excitedly in Italian. One of them led her by the arm toward the laboratory, where Giorno Hals's painting of the pontiff was stretched out on the table. *"Ma che genio!"* the first *professore* said again, and moving aside, he gestured at the pontiff's face.

Where Lizzie thought she had made the worst mistake of her life, removing pigment that had been laid down three hundred years earlier, she now saw an eye that hadn't been there when she had begun working on the painting. It was an eye that had evidently lain hidden underneath the eye that she had wiped off by accident. As Lizzie gazed down disbelievingly at the pontiff's face, the *professori* continued to praise her: what an extraordinary service she had performed on behalf of the Istituto del Restauro! How had she known that the eye she had removed was actually the product of old, clumsy retouching, when some nameless conservator, some *cretino,* some *idioto,* had overpainted? Now everyone could see the eye as the great Flemish artist Giorno Hals had initially intended!

That afternoon, Lizzie met with the director of the institute in his large, sunlight-splashed office. She took a seat in an overstuffed leather armchair, vaguely listening as he told her how extraordinary he thought she was, how she had an intuitive understanding of color and texture, how her hand-eye coordination was perfect—he compared it to perfect pitch in a musician. In rapid Italian which Lizzie understood perfectly, the director concluded, "I would like to offer you a position here on our staff, full-time. Helping out our first- and second-year students."

Lizzie stared at him for a long time. "I'm going to have to say no, signore," she replied in the same rapid Italian. "Actually, I'm going back home to the U.S. I'm pregnant, and my baby is due next summer."

3

∞

When Sarah finished telling her the story of her mother and Masi's relationship, Patrizia sat there for a long time, stunned, her heart thumping unevenly. So many feelings passed through her mind she found it hard to sort them all out; instead, she simply slumped back into the cushions of the couch. As the story was unfolding, Patrizia felt excited and apprehensive, but now that it was over, her stomach hurt and her head was throbbing. For the next few minutes she sat there in silence and disbelief, aware only that her godmother had resumed the story.

"So, Lizzie—I mean, your mother—came back home to the United States," Sarah said softly, "and seven months later, on August twenty-fourth, you were born. And Patrizia, may I tell you something very, very important, that I don't want you ever to forget? I have never seen a child as wanted, or as loved as much, as you were. To your mother, you were the best gift ever. She felt so extraordinarily blessed to have you as her daughter."

"So why didn't she continue her career?" Patrizia asked after a moment, though she already knew the answer.

"Well, your mom felt no matter how much she loved art, and Italy, and working on paintings, that raising a child right is the most important thing there is to do in this life." Sarah smiled. "It wasn't easy for her—it never is for a woman—but Lizzie always said that if you screw up raising your kid, then nothing else is worth anything."

Her mother's quiet heroism, the sacrifices she'd made over the years, sacrifices that she probably didn't even consider to be sacrifices, stunned Patrizia. Lizzie had been offered a job at Italy's leading art institute—and she'd turned it down, returning to America instead to have a child, to give Patrizia life.

Sarah went on with her story. Lizzie had moved back home, and her parents, Patrizia's grandparents, had helped her raise Patrizia. And because there were few if any part-time jobs for art conservators outside of major cities, and Lizzie didn't want to raise a child in an urban area, she had taken the first job she could find, despite being obviously overqualified, as a secretary in the psychology department of the nearby university. When Patrizia's grandparents died, Lizzie had managed to scrape together enough money for a down payment on a small house a few blocks from the house where she'd grown up, where she and Patrizia had moved when Patrizia was four years old.

"And the rest, as they say, is history," Sarah said, attempting to inject a note of lightness into the room's heavy atmosphere.

"So did she ever talk to Masi before she left Rome?"

"No. He found out that she never showed up at the doctor's office in Trastevere, and just as he promised, he cut off all contact with your mother." Sarah smiled sourly. "You can't say Masi wasn't a man of his word. She called him a few times, at school, messages were delivered, but he never called her back. His family was no help whatsoever, even when Lizzie showed up at their doorstep. To them, she was the American girl who had gotten their son into trouble, not the other way around."

"Did she ever contact him after I was born?"

"She sent him a birth announcement," Sarah said dryly. She added, "I thought that was a little much, actually, but your mother insisted he'd want to know the sex of the baby. After that, they had no contact. For your sake and for hers, too. I think it was just too painful for your mother—"

"So why did she have me?" Patrizia asked, her own question taking her by surprise.

"Why?" Sarah hesitated. "It was the seventies. People did their own thing. Your mother loved the idea of you. And somehow the more Masi *didn't* like the idea, the more determined she was to do what *she* wanted to do. At least that's what she told me." She was silent. "I think she didn't tell you about Masi because she didn't want to risk your getting hurt. I know that may be hard for you to understand right now, but maybe someday when you have a child—"

"Did she ever fall in love again?"

"What do you think?" When Patrizia didn't answer, Sarah sighed. "You have to understand. Masi was your mother's first great love. I think maybe unrealistically, she felt if she couldn't love someone like that again, then what was the point?" Sarah fell silent. "I mean, she wasn't a nun, as you know, but I don't think your mother ever met anyone who she felt measured up to him. I mean, you might find that hard to believe after what I've just told you, but—" she didn't complete the thought.

After a silence, Patrizia rose unsteadily. "I'm going to get something to drink. I'll be right back."

In the kitchen, she drank several glasses of tap water in a row while gazing at her reflection in the stainless steel of the stove. Not out of vanity—she looked terrible, frankly, and washed out, considering the amount of crying she'd been doing over the past two weeks—but simply to acknowledge the sheer physical fact of herself. It was true that she'd been thirsty, but she also could not stand the idea of being in that room for a moment longer, with the traces of the story her godmother had just told still darkening the air. She had to move, to shake off the thoughts that were crowding her head.

A few minutes later Patrizia found herself in front of the small bookcase where she and her mother had kept the photographs of Masi for all these years. "Let's put them inside this Italian cookbook," her mother had told her once with a mischievous twinkle in her eye. "That way, we'll always remember where they are."

Very calmly, Patrizia opened the cookbook, found the two photos, ripped them up, and flung the pieces into the garbage.

And yet long after Sarah had returned to Chicago, the excitement Patrizia had felt knowing her father was alive, and living in Rome, and that he'd tried to contact them repeatedly over the years, was now replaced by anger toward her mother. Over the years she had repeatedly asked Lizzie whether her father had ever made any attempts to get in touch with her, and Lizzie had always told her no, he hadn't. When Patrizia asked why, her mother never really answered, though once she'd told her, "Do you know what a narcissist is? It's somebody who thinks only about himself, who's incapable of thinking about other people."

"So what does that have to do with anything?" Patrizia had asked, but Lizzie had changed the subject almost immediately.

What was Lizzie trying to prevent her from knowing? That over the years Masi had been thinking about both of them? That he'd wanted to provide for his child, as well as for the mother of his child? Why hadn't Lizzie wanted to cash any of the checks? Was her pride—and her sense of injury—that great?

It felt wrong to be angry at her mother, whom she loved

and missed more than anything. Instead, Patrizia transferred her hurt and her fury to her father. Masi, her father—the only father she would ever have—hadn't wanted her. It was that simple and that devastating. Money: her father had sent her checks when over the years Patrizia would have sacrificed any amount of money for his attention, his actual physical presence. During the next few weeks she would spend hours trying to analyze her feelings, but without any resolution. Masi hadn't *really* rejected her, had he? After all, was it really possible to reject someone you had never met? Was it possible to reject a person who hadn't been born yet, a person who had threatened to ruin his life, and to destroy his career before it had started? Was it?

Patrizia couldn't get the words out of her head, and she knew she would never forget them:

Il mundo é fatto a scale; c'e chi scende e c'e chi sale.

The world is made of stairs. There are those who go up, and those who go down.

As Sarah was leaving, she had embraced Patrizia tightly, her eyes moist. Then she looked Patrizia in the eye for a long time. "I'm sure you'll do what you have to do," she said.

Several weeks later, when Patrizia learned that she had inherited her mother's monthly pension from the university where she worked, it was easier to make a decision, though in retrospect, she wasn't altogether sure when she first hatched her plan. It might have been when Sarah finished showing her the letters from her father. It might have been in the kitchen, as Patrizia stared at the photographs of her father before consigning them to the garbage. Or it might have been a few days later, when Patrizia, wandering idly through the rooms of the house she'd grown up in, was seized by an anger so powerful she had to take a seat, fearing the intensity of her own emotions.

Again and again, Patrizia returned to the red duffel bag, and to the letters and the aerograms, which were written in surprisingly fluent English. One night, she unfolded one of them and read: *Dear Elizabeth* (Patrizia noted the formality of the "Elizabeth" in the first line, the absence of her mother's pet nickname, "Li"). *This is my fourth letter to you in the past six months, without you replying. Is it too much for me to ask you to cash the checks that I have sent for your and our child's welfare and education? Is it too much for you to provide me with at the very least the minimal information about her?* The signature was black, the stem of the *M* crossed twice, angrily, resembling an arrow inside a bow.

Another aerogram, this one containing a check for five thousand dollars, read tersely: *Even if you do not answer this letter, please start a savings account for our child, and put this money away for her future.* It seemed that every nonanswer from Lizzie simply made Masi even more stubbornly determined to communicate. The last check, Patrizia noticed, was dated February 6, two years earlier. *Dear Elizabeth,* the aerogram read. *From your silence and from the bank telling me again and*

*again that none of the checks I have sent you has ever been cashed,
I am ceasing to contact you any further. Should you wish to communicate with me, here is my address in Rome.*

Several weeks later, after settling her mother's affairs,
Patrizia flew back to New York City. Over the next few
days she informed Holly that she was taking a leave of absence from the gallery, let Lucy know that she should look
for a new roommate, and told Eric that she'd be traveling
to Europe on an extended vacation.

"Is this a nice way of telling me that you don't want to
see me anymore?" Eric asked her. They were eating dinner
at a pizza restaurant not far from Patrizia's apartment.

"Oh, come on, don't be silly," Patrizia replied. She
would miss Eric, but at the same time she was awkwardly,
guiltily aware that he hadn't really figured in her decision to
go abroad. Whenever they had had discussions about their
relationship, it was clear that Eric saw her as part of his future, but Patrizia wasn't sure that her future included him.
Katie wasn't the problem—Eric liked to refer to the relationship between his daughter and Patrizia as a "mutual ad-
miration society." Instead, it was Patrizia's desire for
something more than a boyfriend who was at his happiest
correcting student papers while watching old movies rented
from the downstairs video store, and ordering in Chinese
and Mexican food. At the same time she knew that
thousands of women in New York City wanted just what
she had: a cute, funny, financially secure man who loved
children and had a good job.

"When are you planning on coming back?"

"I don't know," Patrizia said. "Probably in about a month." She was silent. "Eric, I've never been to Europe. And it's a part of me, for better or for worse."

"Will you call me the second you know your phone number?"

"Yes."

"Promise, cross your heart?"

"I promise," she said.

The next few weeks were a blur. Patrizia arranged to store her belongings in a bin out in New Jersey, donated her ficus to the gallery (Lucy had a black thumb as far as plants were concerned), updated her passport, and sat endlessly on hold on the phone, trying to remove her name from the gas, electricity, and cable-TV bills that she and Lucy shared. "Oh God," Lucy exclaimed at one point. "How am I ever going to find a roommate as normal as you? I'm probably going to get some crazy person who hates cigarette smoke."

On a bright, breezy, early August morning with the temperatures in the mid-seventies—ideal flying weather, according to the clerk at the boarding gate—Patrizia Orman boarded Alitalia Flight Sixteen from John F. Kennedy International Airport in New York City for the nearly eight-hour flight to Leonardo da Vinci Airport in Rome, Italy.

∞

It occurred to Patrizia, for the fourth or fifth time that day, just how much she was following in her mother's footsteps.

Limp and worn-out from the flight, the heat inside Rome's sprawling international airport almost made her knees buckle. Seizing her luggage from the slow-moving carousel, she found herself blanking on the Italian words for *train* or *exit,* and so she simply followed the crowd that seemed to be moving in the general direction of a set of elevators.

According the Rome guidebook that Patrizia had tucked into her purse before she left, trains left Fiumicino every hour on the hour for the Stazione Termini, in central Rome. But when she reached the tracks and began studying the schedule of departures, she noticed that the crowd in front of her was milling around agitatedly, and that the waiting train was empty and unlit. One man pounded on the doors without passion, and several people wore expressions of disgust and annoyance on their faces. Then Patrizia overheard an Englishman saying to his wife, almost cheerfully, "Trains are on strike. Happens all the time here, actually."

Nearly an hour later, along with everybody else, Patrizia boarded a bus for downtown Rome.

The bus ride was long and oppressively hot. The air-conditioning wasn't working, the driver announced at the start of the trip, with a shrug that seemed to announce, simply, *These things happen.* Patrizia unbuttoned her top collar, and when this didn't seem to do anything to help relieve her discomfort, she began fanning herself with her passport. New York had been miserable, too, in the weeks before she left—humid, smelly, with a thick wind blowing in off the

Hudson that swirled the garbage in circles around the avenues—but Patrizia had never felt heat as direct and choking as this. Rome in the summertime—though it wasn't as though the guidebooks she'd borrowed from the library hadn't warned her.

As the bus picked up speed, she checked to see if she still had all her luggage with her. She'd packed her bags with as much care and economy as possible, not just a wardrobe for several seasons—she hadn't the slightest idea how long she'd be staying in Italy—but also a small easel whose narrow twin drawers she'd packed with brushes and tubes of oil paint. Under her sweaters she'd laid flat a half-dozen precut canvases, a set of stretcher bars, a box of thirty pushpins, and a field watercolor kit. Relieved that nothing had been squashed or broken in transit, Patrizia focused her attention on the question she'd been asking herself for the past two months:

Was she making a terrible mistake by coming here?

After all, she reminded herself, once the bus pulled into the station in central Rome, it would be so easy to reboard another bus back to Fiumicino, and buy a plane ticket back home. Then again, there was nothing for her in New York except Eric—she had made pretty much certain of that. In fact, she had unconsciously choreographed her life in such a way as to make it almost impossible for her to remain in New York. Now, as the bus lurched onto the highway, Patrizia felt a burst of resolve, mixed with the familiar anger that had accompanied her during almost every waking hour over the past two months. Yes, without a doubt, she had made the right decision coming to Italy. After hearing the story of Lizzie and Masi, it was the only decision she could possibly have made. There were too many questions to which she needed answers, and the only person who could answer these questions lived here, in Rome, just as he'd lived here all his life.

"My father," Patrizia murmured to herself, loud enough so that the man seated beside her stopped chattering into his cell phone for a moment and glanced over curiously in her direction. The words still felt strange on her lips. *My father.*

Patrizia had discussed her trip to Europe with Eric without going into specifics, in part because she wasn't altogether certain of the specifics. "I'm a painter," she said to him. "If you're interested in art, and you don't go to Europe at least once in your life, then there's something the matter with you." She would start off her trip in Italy, she told him, and from there . . . well, she wasn't quite sure herself.

"Maybe you can look up your father while you're over there," Eric had said to her mischievously.

Patrizia smiled. "Right," she said.

She felt uncomfortable telling Eric the truth. She knew that if he found out what she was planning to do in Italy, he would be shocked and probably disappointed. She could only imagine what he would say, words to the effect of, *I thought I knew you, but I realize I don't know you at all.* As the plane had begun its slow descent into Rome, Patrizia realized suddenly that these weren't Eric's words she was imagining, but her own words, spoken to herself. It was true. At age twenty-two, the exact same age her mother had been when she went to study in Italy, she didn't know herself. The Patrizia she *did* know—emotionally detached, fearful, adrift, suspicious of men, *blocked* somehow—she didn't like. She was not a bad person, nor had she ever considered herself to be a vengeful or a deceitful person. But now, to her surprise, she felt possessed of a desire for justice so strong it frightened her.

Patrizia had not told Sarah Bogan about her decision to go to Italy, either. She knew that her godmother would not want to see her risk getting hurt under any circumstances. Moreover, Sarah would be shocked to find out that by a simple act—showing Patrizia the sheaf of letters sent by Masi over the years—she had helped set a plan of revenge in motion.

What am I doing here? Patrizia asked herself. The answer, or at least the answer she had repeated over and over to herself, was simple: she was going to Rome to find her father. But this was the point where the similarities to all her childhood fantasies ended. She had no interest in reconciling with her father. She had no interest in watching fireworks off the bow of an imaginary yacht with him. She was interested only in hurting him, in the same way he had hurt her mother twenty-two years earlier. First she would befriend him, and when he, Masi, trusted her the most, she would somehow betray him, as easily and skillfully as the gypsies had lifted the wallet from Lizzie's handbag nearly twenty-two years earlier. It was the least she owed her mother, and herself. In the weeks following her mother's death, as she kept returning to the faded red duffel bag and the bundle of letters and aerograms marked *ufficio postale,* Patrizia always noted the scrawled address at the bottom of the last letter her father had sent her mother, an address that now, if pressed, she could recite in her sleep:

Masimilliano Caracci. 31 Via Giulia, Rome 90039 Italy.

Forty-five minutes later the bus pulled into a berth outside the Stazione Termini in central Rome, and the engines shut off with a groan. As the passengers began to disembark, pushing and spilling out onto the sidewalk, Patrizia followed, making her way across the Piazza dei Cinquecento, stopping only at a foreign exchange booth to trade her U.S. dollars for lire.

At ten-thirty in the morning, Rome was already baking under the early August sun. The waxy cloud cover over Patrizia's head seemed to toast the pavement beneath her feet. Still, despite her exhaustion, she felt an excitement rising in her chest. She was in Rome, Italy. She was in the city where her mother had fallen in love with her father, and for a time at least, where Masi had fallen in love with her mother. Even though the cracked sidewalk under her feet looked exactly the same as the sidewalk did in front of her apartment in New York, Patrizia was, she realized, standing on an Italian sidewalk. The sky above her head was an Italian sky, the clouds were Italian clouds, the little cars and scooters racing past her were Italian cars and scooters. Even though

she had never been here before, Rome seemed strangely
familiar, and not only because it had provided the backdrop
for a thousand movies she had seen in her life. This city is a
part of me, Patrizia realized to her astonishment. Her father
was Roman, after all, and her roots were in this city. Though
it had been more than two decades since her parents had
met and fallen in love here, Rome probably hadn't changed
in the least; it had simply gotten older.

Patrizia hailed a taxi to her *pensione* in the Campo dei
Fiori. There was no elevator in the small, attractive hotel,
so after checking in, she climbed the four flights to her
room, pausing at each stairwell to rest her heavy suitcases,
remembering to her dismay that she would be sharing a
bathroom with the other guests staying on her floor. But
this didn't matter, because as she reached the second-floor
stairwell, she caught a glimpse out a window of the broad,
chaotic square of the Campo dei Fiore itself. There were
the fruit-and-vegetable and fish stalls, the dark, scowling
statue of Giordano Bruno, the reedy *vicoli,* or side streets,
that led to the Tiber River, and at the far rear of the square,
the weathered restaurant known simply as Alfredo, which,
according to Patrizia's guidebook, specialized in fettuccine
Alfredo.

Patrizia was exhausted, and yet after washing her face
and brushing her teeth, she went back downstairs and asked
the desk clerk for directions to the Piazza Navona.

It felt right, to make her way immediately to the site of
Lizzie and Masi's last, terrible conversation, and twenty

minutes later Patrizia was facing the beautiful Chiesa del Gesù and the Chiesa di Sant'lvo alla Sapienza. And there it was, right in front of her, Bernini's Fontana dei Fiumi, the Fountain of the Four Rivers, with its four muscular stone giants, which Patrizia's mother had returned to again and again, the same fountain that nearly twenty-two years earlier Lizzie had been attempting to paint when she'd been robbed by the gypsy children, which led to her first meeting with Masi.

Being in the actual piazza, the place that had in some ways made possible her existence, as well as her fatherlessness, made Patrizia feel apprehensive. Yet nothing about the Piazza Navona itself suggested the past. Instead, tourists crowded around tables in coffee shops, couples strolled arm in arm around the square's perimeters, voices low in conversation, and a group of boys tossed an old red Frisbee along the sidewalks. The innocence of the Roman morning compared with the harsh farewell between her parents that Sarah Bogan had described gave Patrizia a surge of new anger. Did her father actually believe he could get away with abandoning the mother of his child?

Walking briskly back to her room at the *pensione,* Patrizia changed into her nightgown and fell asleep almost immediately, awakening seven hours later, her stomach growling. But recalling from the various guidebooks that most Roman restaurants didn't open for dinner until at least seven-thirty, she didn't venture outside until nearly nine, when she found a small restaurant around the corner from the Campo dei Fiori. There, she feasted on toasted bread lightly touched with olive oil and fresh wedges of yellow tomato, and for her main course, a thin, ribbonlike pasta dusted with porcini mushrooms and Romano cheese. At the next table, an overweight American couple were discussing what to eat, and she overheard the man saying, "Babydoll, this is Rome. Foodwise, you can't go wrong here."

As Patrizia lingered over her glass of wine, she felt a mixture of emotions—fear, excitement, and even a slight melancholy. After all, the only person missing at this table was Lizzie, Lizzie who, after returning to the United States from Italy, had never once gone back to Europe. She and Patrizia had always discussed going on a mother-daughter jaunt there someday, getting a Eurailpass and just traveling from city to city with no clear-cut itinerary in mind. But there was never enough money, or it was never the right time. Instead, there were short vacations in the car to Canada, to Yosemite, to Chicago, to the Cleveland Art Museum, to the National Gallery in Washington, D.C.

One time, her mother had planned a trip to Florence, but something had come up at the last minute, and she'd had to cancel their plans. To assuage Patrizia's disappointment, Lizzie had concocted something she called Italian Night. As the snow whirled softly around outside in the frigid Midwestern night, Patrizia and her mother sat around the kitchen eating *risotto Milanese* and listening to a singer named Patti Prado bleating from the record player. A few weeks later Lizzie announced out of the blue that it was Paris Night. An hour later she and Patrizia, both wearing silly-looking berets, were dancing around the living room to Juliette Gréco and Serge Gainsbourg records. Most recently, there had been a London Night, with fish and chips served on the business section of the *Chicago Tribune,* and sprinkled with white wine vinegar.

"But just remember," her mother liked to tell Patrizia. "This is no replacement for actually going to these places. This is just me being goofy."

But her mother was by her side, after all, in some ways. A part of her was here. Hadn't Lizzie literally helped restore this city? Hadn't she helped to preserve a small section of the Forum? Wasn't her handiwork reflected somewhere in the stones of the Palatine?

Patrizia lifted her glass silently to the darkly mirrored window of the trattoria. "To you, Mom," she murmured. "I'm here, finally. I just wish right now you were sitting across the table from me."

∞

Jet lag, and the six-hour time difference between Italy and New York City, jolted Patrizia awake at four in the morning. Two hours later she tiptoed out of her room and upstairs to the hotel's roof garden, where she sat watching the sky lighten to purple, then to pink, then to white, and finally to blue. As part of her scheme, she had brought her art supplies with her to Rome, though it hadn't occurred to her that she would ever paint for pleasure, or have the desire to, during her stay. But now, entranced by the early-morning silence of the huge city, Patrizia set about sketching the enormous church across the street from the hotel, with its ornate spires and gargoyles.

For as long as she could remember, her teachers had considered Patrizia a precociously talented painter. Like a lot of children, she enjoyed drawing simple shapes and figures—suns, flowers, trees—but at age six, she had startled her mother by copying Gauguin's *Nevermore* from an art book that Lizzie had left lying around the living room. Lizzie took one look at her daughter's drawing, and entered her into local art classes. It was only later that Patrizia realized that the beginning of her art education coincided with the last time she'd ever seen Lizzie's favorite gold bracelet, the one that had been passed down to her by her grandmother. It was Lizzie who later reluctantly encouraged Patrizia to attend art school. "You have a gift," she said simply. "I would have given just about anything to have your talent when I was seventeen."

At art school, her professors had also predicted great things for Patrizia, but when she arrived in New York, she found herself painting less and less. It was almost as if finding herself alone, in a strange city, she was scared to paint. The paintings Patrizia did manage to complete were technically proficient, but lacking in any warmth, or passion. Frustrated, she had considered quitting painting altogether. Holly had told her, wisely, "I'm not sure that's your decision to make."

"What do you mean?" Patrizia had asked.

"You're an artist," Holly said slowly, "which means that

your painting tells you what to do, and not the other way around." In the months before her mother's death, several galleries across the country had expressed an interest in her work—did Patrizia have a portfolio? An agent?—but when Lizzie died, she seemed to have lost any desire to paint.

Now, as Rome started coming to life in the broad piazzas and narrow streets below her, Patrizia packed up her watercolors and pad and returned to her hotel room, where she laid out her outfit carefully—blue jeans, sandals, and a white V-necked T-shirt—and then dressed in silence. Before leaving the *pensione,* she glanced at herself approvingly in the lobby mirror: now she looked like the essence of an American tourist, no different from thousands of other college-age girls visiting Rome for the first time.

The sensation of being alone and adrift in a foreign city was strangely exciting. No one knew her name; she was responsible to no one; she could do, or be, whatever she wanted. She could recall feeling this way only once before, when she had driven to Florida during her senior year of college to visit a friend. Stopping at roadside motels in the late afternoon whenever she was tired of driving, she remembered the mixture of fear and delight she'd felt when she realized that if she didn't telephone anyone, then no one in the world would know where she was. One night, reminding herself of this fact once again, Patrizia had panicked. With enormous relief, she dialed her mother's number, and when Lizzie answered, Patrizia almost shouted, "It's me!"

This time, Patrizia didn't feel remotely panicked. She

had counted on her anonymity. In fact, it was central to her plan.

At nine in the morning, it was already close to ninety degrees outside—a thick, wet, baking summer heat. August in Rome. A time, according to the guidebooks she had scanned, when most shops and restaurants shut down, and when most of the Roman population, or at least those people who could afford it, fled the city for a cooler climate, either the beaches or the mountains. Taking out her city map, Patrizia traced the route she would take to the Via Giulia. Map in hand, she made her way down the Via dei Giubbonari, onto the Via delle Botteghe Oscure, past the Chiesa Santa Maria in Aracoeli, and onto the Via dei Fori Imperiali. Though it was a short trip, by the time she had reached the Via Giulia, her neck and collar were moist with perspiration. The Romans she passed along the way seemed to be bearing up under the heat just as poorly as she was, the workmen on scaffolding sweating under their caps, the straps of women's bras clinging limply to their ribs and shoulders. Other Romans seemed to have surrendered to the summertime: the two middle-aged women Patrizia had passed dangling their bare feet in the cool water of an ornate Roman fountain before a policeman ordered them to stop; the cluster of teenage boys who ripped off their shirts when she walked past them. *"Te adoro,"* one of the boys had shouted at her, "and I want you to love me back!" but Patrizia kept walking.

The Via Giulia was a broad avenue that to Patrizia's

surprise had no sidewalk at all on one side, just a small six-inch-high curb where pedestrians could find shelter from speeding cars and scooters. There was a gray, drowsy feeling in the air. The neighborhood was nearly deserted, and most of the stores and restaurants that she passed were closed for August. Cars were parked haphazardly on the opposite sidewalk, their snub noses pressed in against the side of the buildings, parking spaces in Rome evidently at a premium.

For the first time Patrizia felt a wave of anxiety, and even a sense of dread. She stopped to peer at her reflection in the mirrored window of a small bakery, this time not to see whether or not she looked authentically American, but to see if she looked pretty. She did. The dusty Roman heat had brought a flush to her cheeks, and a sharpness to her features.

Why in the world does it matter if I look pretty for my father? Patrizia asked herself.

By now, she had gradually become aware of the street numbers. There was number 25 Via Giulia. There was number 29. Across the avenue was number 30. And then Patrizia was standing directly in front of number 31, with its half circle of discreet red letters reading *GALLERIA MASIMILLI-ANO CARACCI* splashed across the glass.

Obviously, Masimilliano Caracci had done well for himself over the years.

Patrizia stood outside her father's gallery for a long time, gazing at the sharp red letters. It was as if she were examining a face, the face that Masi showed off to the world. The sign on the door announced that the gallery was closed, but she

rang the bell anyway, and was surprised when almost immediately a beautiful dark-haired woman opened the door.

"*Buongiorno,*" Patrizia said, and she hesitated. "*Parla inglese?*"

The woman's face relaxed. "Oh my God, do I ever
speak English," she said. "I'm from Vermont originally. I
can't tell you how nice it is to hear someone speaking a
language I can actually understand." She hesitated. "But I'm
afraid the gallery is closed all this month. The entire city of
Rome shuts down in August, in case you were wondering
why it's such a ghost town around here."

"I was actually looking for Mr. Caracci," Patrizia said.

"Oh, Masi's not around." The woman uttered his name
with a casual intimacy that gave Patrizia pause. "But is there
something I can help you with?"

"Do you know if he'll be in sometime later?"

For the first time the woman frowned. "Is this a pro-
fessional thing or a personal thing?"

Patrizia hadn't counted on meeting anybody else at the
gallery, and she found herself grappling for the right answer.
"Personal," she said at last. "Actually, Masi's an old friend
of my mother's. She told me that if I was ever in Rome, I
should look him up." The ease with which this partial lie
rolled off her tongue surprised her. "Anyway, I'm not one
of those people who makes it a habit to call up people I've
never met when I'm in a new city, but then this morning I
said to myself, why not?"

Whatever she had said seemed to do the trick, since the

woman seemed to grow noticeably friendlier, though when she told Patrizia that Masi was at his summer place in the Italian coastal town of Porto Ercole, on the Argentario Peninsula, until early September, Patrizia was aware of a familiar crushed sensation in her chest. September. That was nearly three weeks away. She could not wait until September. It felt to her almost as though her father had abandoned her yet again.

"Since I'm here, would you mind terribly much if I looked around Mr. Caracci's gallery?" Patrizia asked.

The woman hesitated. "I shouldn't—" She didn't finish. "Oh, I guess it's okay," she said finally. "My name's Becky, by the way . . ."

There were four gray-carpeted rooms in all, each one larger than the next, and each one dominated by raised skylights. The final room opened onto an enclosed garden draped with plants and vines, and occupied by a trickling fountain: two sleek marble dolphins spouting water from their upraised mouths. Patrizia now remembered the story Sarah Bogan had told her, how in Florence, Masi had told Lizzie how much he detested museums, how in his opinion they made all art seem dead and lifeless. Despite the absence of any paintings on the walls, Patrizia couldn't help but admire the vitality of Masi's gallery—the plants, the water, the high ceilings, and the skylights that seemed to let in the Roman morning rather than shut it out. As she wandered back through the gallery, Becky trailed behind her. "Masi's having a huge opening on September twentieth," she said.

"Young artists from all around the world. That's why the walls are so empty right now."

"It doesn't really feel like a gallery, does it?" Patrizia said, but at that moment a telephone rang distantly, and when Becky scurried off to answer it, Patrizia wandered over to the reception area, a cubicle to the right of the doorway. It was simply adorned: an old wooden desk, a potted plant, a credit-card machine, and stacks of papers.

"So quiet you can't even imagine," Becky was saying into the phone. Then, in a more concerned voice: "How are you feeling today?"

Behind the reception area was a broad cherrywood desk, and though it had no nameplate, Patrizia knew who it belonged to. Her eyes took in her father's belongings: A gold fountain pen. A gold clock. A silver letter opener. Paper clips, thumbtacks, a stack of business cards, a portable computer. Then, leaning in closer, she saw the enormous stamped manila envelope about to be forwarded to Signore Masimilliano Caracci at his summer address in Porto Ercole.

"No," Becky was saying into the phone. "I would love to, but my parents will still be here. I thought I'd take them to Ostia Antica or something. My mother wants to go to Pompeii, but it's too far and too hot in this weather."

Having memorized the address, Patrizia turned just in time to hear Becky say, "Okay, Masi. I love you, too. Don't wear yourself out too much, okay? I'll see you in a couple of weeks."

Okay, Masi. Her father! All this time Becky had been

talking to her father! The indirect proximity to him thrilled Patrizia, and at the same time confused her. *I love you, too? I'll see you in two weeks?* No wonder Becky had sounded so offhand when she said his name. Masi this, Masi that. Were they married? Patrizia wondered. Engaged? Was Becky having an affair with him? Patrizia made her way toward the door.

"Oh," Becky said into the phone with a small laugh. "What's the matter with me? There's somebody here right now to see you." She cupped her hand over the phone. "I'm sorry," she called out to Patrizia, "what did you say your name was again?"

Patrizia, who hadn't given a name, was already halfway out the door. "Don't worry, I'll be back another time," though when she reached the sidewalk of the Via Giulia, she ran without looking back.

∞

"Could you tell me the best way to get from Rome to Porto Ercole?" Patrizia asked the desk clerk at her *pensione*.

It was late in the day, and Patrizia was bone-tired. Catching her breath after leaving her father's gallery, she found herself desperate for someplace restful—a museum or a quiet piazza—and checking her guidebook, she set off for Aventine Hill and the Protestant Cemetery, where she had spent most of the afternoon, returning home along the river to the Campo dei Fiori. Now she was damp with perspiration and her legs and feet hurt from all the walking she'd done. Paolo, the desk clerk with the formal but slightly ironic manner—since her arrival, he had addressed Patrizia as "madam," bowing as he said it—was busy conversing with another man behind the desk, and now he looked up. "It is not so easy, madam, unfortunately. Do you have a car?"

Patrizia shook her head. "Though I guess I could rent one, couldn't I?"

Paolo grimaced. "Even if you don't value your life, madam, I value it. Once you get outside of Rome, the driving is fine. It is getting out of Rome that is the problem." He hesitated. "Do you have a place to stay in Porto Ercole? Can I make a reservation anyplace for you?"

"I would appreciate that," Patrizia said slowly. She didn't trust her command of Italian, and wasn't sure how long her luck in finding people who spoke English would hold out. "I can't pay all that much," she added apologetically. "If you know of someplace to stay that's cheap—"

"Don't worry, madam, I will take care of you." Paolo picked up the phone, dialed, and spoke in rapid Italian, keeping his eye on Patrizia the whole time. Hanging up, he scrawled the name of a hotel on a piece of scrap paper, which he presented to her.

"*Grazie.*" She pocketed the piece of paper. Then: "What about trains or buses that run to Porto Ercole?"

There was no direct train or bus service between Rome and the Argentarian coast, Paolo informed her (and even if there had been, he reminded her, the nation's conductors were on strike). "We should have thought of this perhaps before making you a reservation." He shrugged. "You could always hire a car."

"But that's probably very expensive, right?"

Paolo pursed his lips. Clearly he was accustomed to rich Americans who were able to afford whatever they wanted. "Yes," he said, adding, slightly helplessly, "Madam"—another faint bow—"it is not so cheap anywhere these days. We are talking two hundred, three hundred dollars, American, and that is one way."

"I don't think I can afford that," Patrizia said softly after a moment.

"You have no friend who could take you? No boyfriend, or uncle, or nephew?"

For the first time the other young man behind the desk spoke, addressing both Paolo and Patrizia. "If she had a nephew, he would be five years old! Too young to have a driver's license!" Indicating Paolo, the young man added to Patrizia, "He thinks he knows a word like *nephew* and he is the best English speaker in the world! But it's a *lousy* thing!"

He was a strikingly handsome young man in his early twenties with short black hair and a shadowy complexion, though it was the turquoise color of his eyes that Patrizia found most arresting. As the two men began talking suddenly in rapid Italian, she backed away and took a seat on the bench in the lobby of the *pensione*. She felt as alone and as undefended as she had ever felt in her life. Then her helplessness turned abruptly to anger, directed toward herself. What was she doing here in Italy? What kind of absurd plan was this anyway? The answer was: It was no plan at all. It was sheer impulsiveness, sheer wrongheadedness. Hadn't Lucy, her roommate, warned her not to make any major decisions following her mother's death? "You can end up doing some really nutty things," Lucy had told her, adding that when her father died, she'd gotten engaged to a man she didn't love "just so I could feel I belonged to a family again," though fortunately she'd broken it off in time. Being here in Italy was a mistake. Patrizia's shins ached, her socks itched. She was hungry and thirsty. What was she expecting anyway? Had she expected simply to arrive in Rome, and there her father would be, waiting for her? A tear slid down her face, and she didn't have the strength to wipe it away.

"Signorina," she heard suddenly, and when Patrizia looked up, the second man behind the desk, the one with the blue eyes, was gazing down at her with a worried expression. "Please don't—" and he didn't finish. "I hate that this is—" The young man started again. "I can take you there, okay?"

"Take me to where?"

"Monte Argentario."

"But I can't afford to hire a car."

"Later. We will worry about that together later, right? Now, I have to tell you it is not a fantastic car, but it will get us to where we are going, and that is the most important thing."

"I don't even know who you are——"

The young man put out his hand. "Andrea Pisanelli."

Behind the desk, Paolo broke in. "Andrea is okay. You have my word for that. He is dependable."

"The problem, however? It is that I cannot drive you there today." Delivering this piece of news, Andrea's manner seemed almost tragic. "My car is making a funny noise in the engine like screaming, and it will not be ready until too late tonight. Tomorrow, early, is that okay with you?"

The dirty blue station wagon was waiting on the curb outside the *pensione* at seven-thirty the next morning, and when Patrizia appeared with her suitcases, Andrea seized them from her, storing them in the trunk, then opening up the passenger door and indicating to her that she should climb in. Despite the cut rate she was getting, she was already feeling agitated about the cost of the trip, though Andrea, who had retaken the driver's seat, quickly put her at her ease. "Signorina, how did you sleep last night?"

"Fine, thank you," though in truth, jet lag and anxiety and an air conditioner that refused to chill the room had kept her awake half the night.

"I don't know your name." Andrea posed it as a question.

"Patrizia. Patrizia Orman."

"You are American, right? But you have an Italian

name?" He didn't wait for her to answer. "I could tell you are American immediately," he added comfortably.

"Oh yeah, how?"

"I don't know. The way that your blue jeans fit you. I like it very much. Here in Europe, you know, the blue jeans always look a little funny. The way Italian people wear them, and French people, too? There is something always a little off, something always a little strange, an inch here, an inch there. But you, your blue jeans fit you so very, very well."

Embarrassed, suppressing a laugh, Patrizia managed to say, only, "Thanks, I guess."

When Andrea had offered to drive her to Porto Ercole, she had imagined a long, sleek car, an ink-black Mercedes, maybe, with footrests and a reading lamp. After all, wasn't she paying dearly for the privilege of a chauffeur-driven car? But the interior of the station wagon was cramped and shabby, and smelled of stale cigarette smoke, and the engine made a faint jangling sound. Opera sounded softly from the radio. As the car sped north on the highway, she took the opportunity to glance out the window at the passing landscape. The greenery of the countryside came as a welcome relief from the clogged streets and inertia of Rome in the summertime. Outside the city, past the workmen's neighborhoods, past the modern industrial complexes with their names spelled out in colorful neon script—Olivetti and Fiat, among others—Patrizia noticed fields dotted with grazing sheep and goats. To her surprise, instead of looking out the window, she found herself studying the back of Andrea's head, the slight groove along the back of his neck, the hairs there like a slanting rain. He was the most attractive man she'd met in a long time, and she felt an unfamiliar pull in her stomach.

"So this is your first trip to Italy?" Andrea asked. Patrizia could see the top of his dark glasses in the mirror.

"Yes."

"And so far—is it okay for you?"

"So far, it is," she replied. She didn't want to say very much, in part because she sensed that it was a strain for him to speak English, and in part because his attractiveness intimidated her slightly. Presently, she began to notice black-skinned women on the sides of the road dressed in skimpy outfits, and in her halting Italian, she asked Andrea what the women were doing there. To her surprise, he turned around, his eyes bold. "They are prostitutes," he said. "They embarrass this country. I am sorry if they embarrass you."

"It's okay, Andrea," Patrizia said. "I didn't know."

He quickly changed the subject. "So Paolo tells me that you know no one in Porto Ercole."

"You and Paolo sure talked a lot about me."

"Paolo is my younger brother. I love him. He is lousy sometimes, but . . ." His voice trailed off.

So that was how Andrea already knew so much about Patrizia. "You are as beautiful as Paolo told me that you were," he went on. "Of course I saw this yesterday myself when I met you."

Suspicious of Mediterranean charm—look what had happened to her mother, after all—Patrizia ignored the compliment. "I'm just . . . a painter," she said. "And I hear that Porto Ercole is very beautiful, so I just thought I would see what it looked like."

"You don't know a soul, not anybody, in Porto Ercole, and you are just showing up there and saying, 'This is me, here I am'?" Andrea sounded disbelieving. He didn't wait for Patrizia to answer. "I admire your courage." He stared at the road for a moment, before nimbly passing the car in front of him. "This is another reason I like Americans. You have the courage that says, 'So what?' Italy is a much more closed society than America. But it is right sometimes to say—you know?—so what? To follow your heart. Right?"

To her surprise, Patrizia found herself talking to Andrea in an easy way that reminded her of how she used to talk with Eric. It was the first time she'd thought about Eric since arriving in Italy, and she felt a stab of guilt. Hadn't she promised to call him the moment she arrived? Yes, she'd told him she would, but overcome by the sights and sounds of a new country, as well as by her mission, she'd forgotten all about her promise.

"I would like to go to America sometime," Andrea was saying. "Of course I would need a very good reason to go." He hesitated. "A girl I loved, maybe."

"And do you love anybody here?" Patrizia heard herself asking, then kicked herself for asking such a familiar question. What was the matter with her?

There was a silence, then Andrea caught her eyes in the rearview mirror for several seconds, before looking away. "I do not really know the answer to that," he said finally. Then: "Will you pardon me if we stop for a moment?"

A moment later he pulled the car into a narrow crescent on the side of the road, abruptly opened the door, and got out. Taking a pack of cigarettes from his shirt pocket, he plunged one into his mouth, and cupping his hands around the tip, lit it, and inhaled deeply, almost sorrowfully, his back to Patrizia. Presently, he turned around and tapped on her window. She rolled it down. "I smoke and I know Americans are very puritan about cigarettes," Andrea said. "So—"

"It's okay, I really don't mind the smell all that much," Patrizia broke in.

"The times I smoke it's like the cigarette is like a cork and I am like a bottle. You know?" Patrizia didn't, really, but she nodded anyway. "There's something that I want to say," Andrea went on, "but I can't, or I am nervous or scared about saying it. So instead of speaking, I put this"—he fumbled for the words—"this lousy cork in my mouth and I smoke it."

"Really, it's okay," Patrizia said as Andrea stubbed out his cigarette and climbed back into the front seat. Daringly, she added, "Why—what did you want to say to me that you were scared to?"

Andrea shrugged. "I can tell you the next time, okay?"

Patrizia squirmed in her seat, then fell silent, dozing off slightly and awakening to the fresh smell of sea salt through her open window. The terrain up north was flatter than in Rome, and presently she noticed the small, nearly hidden sign for Porto Ercole, and the tall trees, planted with geometrical precision, lining the road. Several miles later, as the station wagon began to climb a steep hill, Patrizia made out a cluster of sailboats blooming through a stand of trees, with more boats tied up behind them. To her left there appeared a mountain, beyond which there appeared, magically, a perfectly enclosed oval of blue water ringed by houses, apartment buildings, shops, and restaurants.

"That is the Tyrrhenian Sea," Andrea remarked. It was the first thing he had said in nearly an hour, though Patrizia had caught him glancing at her several times in the rearview mirror. "It changes color even while you are looking at it. The Romans used to call this port Portus Herculis."

Patrizia's heart took a leap. It was official now: she was in the same town as her father. She gazed out the window, only half listening to what Andrea was telling her: *The king of the Netherlands comes here sometimes . . . he just hops out of his yacht and into a waiting car, up the mountain to his villa . . . the best part of Porto Ercole are the white sandy beaches, where you can go sailing and rowing and motorboating and swimming . . . there are grottoes you can reach only from the sea . . . you see the fortifications up on the hill, used in the war against the Spanish . . .*

The center of Porto Ercole was crowded with tourists, and as Andrea steered the car down the small, winding streets through the center of town, he was forced to apply his brakes again and again, before coasting gently down the hill to a road facing the water, which was crowded with fish vendors. "What is the name of your hotel again?" he asked.

Patrizia was far too preoccupied to answer at once. She was busy staring out the car window at every man she saw on the street. There was a man in light blue shorts and an oxford button-down shirt, holding a shopping bag, walking smartly up the steep hill: was that Masi? What about the man crouched in front of the *gelateria,* his face and expression averted, a smoldering cigarette between his fingers, and a bunch more stubbed out on the ground below his bare feet: was that Masi? The man now piloting his rowboat past several other bobbing rowboats: was that Masi? The man with his arm around the little girl's shoulder, the little girl chewing a blue Popsicle, the two of them heading home in wet bathing suits—was that Masi?

Then again, for all she knew, Masi had gone back to Rome. Perhaps they had passed each other on the highway and not even known it. Or perhaps Masi had gotten tired of Porto Ercole, and instead driven north to Lake Como, or to Lake Garda, or to Venice, or to Umbria, or to Pisa . . .

Patrizia gave Andrea the name of her *pensione,* and a moment later he slowed down in front of a small, brightly colored waterfront hotel, got out, and brought her suitcases into the lobby.

"How much do I owe you?" she asked when they were back on the sidewalk.

With his lips pursed, Andrea touched his index finger to his forehead and pretended to think. "What day is it today?"

"Thursday," Patrizia replied, puzzled. Then: "Why?"

"Patrizia, there is a rule in Italy that not many tourists know about. All car trips in Italy that take place on Thursday afternoons are free of charge."

"No—" she started to say.

"It is a little-known rule. Imagine what would happen if the whole world found out about it! Terrible things! The Italian economy would go bankrupt in two weeks, I know it! You *can* do one thing for me, though."

"What?" she asked, still overcome by Andrea's generosity.

"Will you have dinner with me tonight? Or can I see you tomorrow sometime?"

Startled, Patrizia blurted out, "But don't you have to go back to Rome?"

"You don't understand, do you?"

"Understand what?"

Andrea knit his hands before him, and to Patrizia he looked like a guilty child. "I admit to you, I am not a driver by profession. I am a university student with a car that is not fantastic. Paolo tells me there is a beautiful girl in his hotel, and she is my type, too. He also says she has gotten no phone calls from any men—and a man calls usually very quickly to see if the girl that he loves has gotten safely to where she was traveling—and she has no boyfriend in Porto Ercole, so I draw a conclusion that she is free." He cleared his throat. "Then I think to myself, I would like to leave Rome and go to the Monte Argentario, too, along with the girl." Andrea was silent. "Do you hate me now for deceiving you a little?"

Patrizia gazed at him, charmed by his maneuvering. No wonder the station wagon was in such bad shape; it wasn't a rental car at all. In some ways, they were alike, she and Andrea: both of them pretending to be other people. A vision of Eric floated through her head, then vanished as quickly as it had appeared. "I don't hate you in the slightest, Andrea," she said at last, feeling an unexpected beat of excitement in her chest.

"So dinner tonight? Or breakfast tomorrow?"

"I can't," she said after a moment, reluctantly. "There's a lot I have to do—"

"What about lunch tomorrow?"

"Tomorrow's not good at all."

"Why, what are you doing? You tell me you didn't know any people in Porto Ercole."

"I don't. Know anybody. I just have"—Patrizia couldn't explain—"all this stuff I have to do."

Andrea looked hurt. "Okay—I get the message. Just tell me, okay?"

"Andrea, it's not like that at all," Patrizia said, seeing that she'd hurt his feelings.

"So why won't you spend time with me, then?"

"Okay, I'll meet you for breakfast tomorrow," Patrizia said, barely recognizing her own voice.

"Good. I will pick you up at your hotel at eight or nine."

"But where will you stay tonight?" she called after him.

Andrea turned around. "Me? I don't care. Whatever hotel has a room for me. I will not be able to sleep anyway now that I know you."

What had she just gotten herself into? As Patrizia watched Andrea back away, fumble behind him for the door of the station wagon, and slide back inside, she felt a strange mixture of desire and guilt. Eric—where was Eric in all this? The image of Eric was replaced by the image of Andrea's incandescent eyes, his mixture of shyness and boldness. The image of both men was just as abruptly replaced by a mental picture of Masi, her father, twenty-two years old, posing with his hands in both pockets, his dark thin face looking displeased under the gaze of Lizzie's camera. Masi: that's why she was here, after all.

After leaving her luggage in her room, Patrizia changed into shorts and a T-shirt, and went out to explore her father's town. She made her way along the narrow road that ran alongside the waterfront, entranced by the smell of ocean salt that clung to the pilings. In this respect, she was still very much a Midwesterner, still fascinated by the presence of any water that wasn't a lake, any water that didn't have obvious limits or boundaries. The sound of oars and luffing sails and rattling halyards competed with the slap of water against the low seawall facing the ocean. Still, the harbor water did not look hospitable. Andrea was right about the colors of the Tyrrhenian. It was green in some spots, brown in others, a funny radiant pink in still others. Sea grass ground up by outboard motors mixed with fatty-looking clumps of foam.

After stopping at an open-air restaurant, where she downed two slices of *pizza bianca,* and to give herself energy in this Mediterranean heat, a double espresso, Patrizia circled back into the center of town, past a row of local stores. There was a *fruttivendolo,* where you could buy fresh fruit and vegetables, a *latteria,* with its bottles of fresh milk and cream and its tubs of fresh cheese, and a *panificio,* with its rough dark loaves of bread in the window, spreading out from dark straw baskets.

To Patrizia's surprise, the population of Porto Ercole seemed to have tripled in just the fifteen minutes it had taken her to walk from one end of the shore road to the other. The late-afternoon summer stillness had given way to a sudden explosion of people, most of them walking without purpose or direction. The crowd consisted of families, men, women, and impeccably dressed children, walking casually in groups along the docks.

Suddenly she remembered: this was the *passeggiata,* a tradition according to which every evening at dusk, Italian families promenaded along the streets of their towns. She had just extracted her guidebook from her purse—she wanted to see if it had anything more to say about *passeggiatas*—when she caught sight of him.

It wasn't that Patrizia recognized him from the two curling photographs that had made their home for so long in Lizzie's cookbook. Masi, of course, was no longer the young man in the dark leather jacket, or the overserious Roman boy who didn't like the idea of getting his picture taken in

the Piazza Navona. Nor could Patrizia have recognized him
from Lizzie's vague descriptions of him over the years. Nor
was it the fact that he, Masi, was one of the few Italians on
the narrow streets of Porto Ercole who didn't seem to be a
part of the *passeggiata,* and who was, instead, making his way
against the crowds, carrying two white plastic sacks of what
looked from a distance like groceries, bottled water, bread,
and wine.

It wasn't from pictures or anecdotes that she realized she
had found her father. Her recognition came from a stranger
source: Patrizia recognized herself in him, and him in herself.
Everything about Masi—the casual gait, the slight curvature
in his hips, the angle of his shoulders—she had always assumed were qualities unique to her. Staring at her father as
he made his way along the waterfront, his head slightly low-
ered, his baggy shorts flapping, his T-shirt weakly billowing
in the wind—was like seeing herself within a man. How
was this possible? Men were men and women were
women—completely different. How could they be such a
part of each other in this way?

Patrizia continued staring as Masi paused to exchange a
few words with an acquaintance he'd bumped into halfway
up the hill. Next to this taller acquaintance, she saw that
Masi was shorter than she'd imagined, no taller than five-
eight or five-nine. Despite his forty-four years, he didn't
seem to have taken on any of the slowness or thickening of
middle age. If anything, he seemed too thin, almost frail in
appearance.

There was another quality about him that Patrizia wasn't able to put her finger on until much later, when she was able to reduce it to its simplest component. It was the thing about Masi that amazed her more than anything.

Her father was human. He was real. He was not an invention, not a figure frozen in photographs, not someone mentioned casually in conversation by Sarah, or by her mother. He was real, and he was standing only fifty feet away from her. For the first time ever Patrizia realized that no matter what she had thought about this man over the years, the picture of him that she had painted in her head had nothing to do with an actual human being.

The tears that came to her eyes then took her by surprise. As her father made his way up an angular rise in the road, Patrizia did not even consider following him. No, that part would come tomorrow. Instead, she remained frozen in place, gazing at Masi as he disappeared from sight.

That night, in her *pensione,* gazing out the window at the reflections of light on the dark harbor, Patrizia was forced to remind herself why she had come to Italy in the first place, why she had interrupted her life in New York to travel first to Rome, and now to Porto Ercole. The image of Masi on the sidewalk, casual and self-sufficient in his shorts and sandals, disappeared. Now this image was replaced by the same image of a man ambling up a hill, carrying groceries, a man leading a life without any responsibilities whatsoever, a life without the woman and the child he had discarded twenty-two years earlier.

And she reminded herself, too, of the power that Masi had always had over her life, even though he lived thousands of miles away. His presence was behind every choice she had made, or been incapable of making, in her life. Without him, she might not have grown up where she had. She might have grown up in Rome, or, for that matter, in Porto Ercole. When Patrizia thought back on her childhood, she pictured a single mother working hard to raise a single child. The loneliness of that memory—that, too, was thanks to Masi.

And now the power that her father had wielded over her all her life was finally, after all these years, going to end.

4
∞

She had had a surprisingly difficult time coming up with a name.

Frankly, it was much easier to consider what names she *wasn't* going to use. Sophia, as in Sophia Loren, the name that had come automatically to mind, wasn't a possibility—too obvious. The same went for Gina, or Anna, or any similar name that could be associated with one of the famously exotic, fiery-eyed actresses whose films Patrizia and Lizzie had watched on late-night television during the long, cold Wisconsin winters. Then she realized that the name she chose didn't necessarily have to be Italian in origin. She was in Italy pretending to be a tourist, right? (Well, in fact she *was* a tourist.) And after all, hadn't she always complained to her mother how much she hated having been christened

"Patrizia"? Hadn't she always minded that growing up, surrounded by Krisses, Ambers, Ninas, and Jennifers, her name
had set her apart from her friends? Wasn't this her chance
to rechristen herself with the name she'd always wanted?

But it wasn't until Patrizia was in the plane going to
Rome that she had heard a flight attendant summoning one
of the passengers. "Will Anna Dineen please make herself
known to a member of the flight crew?" the smoothly pro-
fessional voice asked, repeating the message a few minutes
later. Almost unconsciously, Patrizia decided that from that
moment on that she would be known, in Italy at least, as
Anna Dineen.

With Andrea, her name hadn't mattered. After he
dropped her off in Porto Ercole, Patrizia had assumed she
would never see him again. Delighted that this wasn't the
case, she was glad that she'd told him her real name. What
did Andrea have to do with her father, anyway? Their paths
would never cross, at least not if Patrizia could help it.

All these various issues of identity passed through her
mind the next morning as she assembled her supplies. A few
oil paints, a palette and palette knife, a canvas and tacks, as
well as the small portable wooden easel that she'd packed in
her suitcase. With her art supplies in tow, Patrizia headed
downstairs into the lobby of her hotel. She was deciding
what to do next—grab a cup of coffee or wait outside for
Andrea—when to her surprise, she spotted him reclining on
the wicker couch in the lobby. Even more surprising, he
looked nothing like the college student she'd met yesterday.

Instead, he was dressed casually and smartly, a lightweight sweater tied around his neck.

Andrea sprang to his feet when he caught sight of Patrizia. "I told you, it would be impossible for me to sleep with you now in my life," he said, kissing her on both cheeks. He added, almost proudly, "I have been up since five-thirty this morning."

Patrizia could feel herself blushing. When was the last time she had blushed? Had she, in fact, ever blushed? As Andrea took her suitcases and portable easel from her, she concealed her nervousness behind a brisk manner. "So where shall we eat breakfast?" she asked once they were outside.

"Why not back to my hotel? I was lucky—they had a cancellation and I have a cottage to myself. Very private, very pretty. And you must not worry," Andrea teased, noting the expression on her face. "They serve the breakfast next to the swimming pool, not in my bedroom. Come— it will feel good to walk."

Fifteen minutes later Patrizia was seated underneath a vast, snow-white sun-drenched umbrella beside the deep blue swimming pool of the Pellicano Hotel, eating fresh halves of papaya and *cornetti,* and washing them both down with the best freshly squeezed orange juice she had ever tasted. Clearly the Pellicano Hotel catered to a moneyed international crowd, and to Patrizia's surprise, Andrea seemed very much at home there. When the bill came, he ignored her protests and instructed the waiter to charge the breakfast to his room. "I don't want you paying for me," Patrizia said.

Andrea made a dismissive sound. "You are my guest in this country. I will take care of you while you are here—all right?"

"Andrea, I can pay my own way."

"Of course you can. It is just that I will not permit you to. Someday when I am in America you can buy me a Coca-Cola and a Big Mac and a Beanie Baby. Then we will be square, okay? Until then, you are my guest." Andrea paused. "Patrizia, I am very fortunate to come from a successful family. My father is rich. But *i soldi non sono importante*. I don't want money to be anything between us."

"But what about Paolo?" she couldn't help saying.

"Paolo what?"

"Well, I mean—" Now Patrizia was embarrassed. "Paolo works at a hotel. Behind the desk. But you just said your family was—"

"Yes." Andrea was gazing at her, smiling. "My family also owns that hotel. They own three hotels in all, two in Rome, one in Todi." He shrugged. "Everybody works. And Paolo works harder than most people."

Afterward, Patrizia and Andrea walked wordlessly down to the edge of the harbor, and at one point Andrea gripped her hand in his. As they stood watching the fishing boats puttering out for that day's work, Patrizia glanced down at her wristwatch. "I have to go," she said softly.

"Go where?"

Patrizia couldn't very well explain. "I just have to go, that's all. Paint," she added, almost helplessly.

"Must you do that, really?"

She wanted nothing more than to remain where she was—on the dock overlooking the harbor, with the sun brightening, the smells of the harbor beginning to infuse the town, and Andrea's hand in hers, but she couldn't. Not if she wanted her plan to succeed.

"So when do I see you next?" Andrea asked.

"Tomorrow," Patrizia said.

Andrea was insistent. "Tomorrow when?"

They made a plan to meet for lunch at her hotel at two o'clock. Andrea insisted on carrying Patrizia's bags back to her *pensione,* and when it was time to say good-bye, he reached into his pants pocket, extracted his cigarettes, and fired one up. Patrizia laughed.

"What?" Andrea asked roughly.

"I'm just laughing, that's all."

"And what are you laughing at? Not at me, I hope."

"I'm laughing because you're smoking," she said, "and yesterday you told me that you smoke instead of saying what's on your mind."

Andrea gazed into her eyes, a moment later tossing his half-smoked cigarette to the pavement. "Okay, you win," he said, sighing. "Here is the thing: I want to kiss you on your lips. I have wanted to do that since I saw you in Rome. And I do not know whether to ask you if I can do that, or whether I should be very, very impolite and just do it."

Patrizia was silent. "Why don't you just do it."

"You mean right now? Right here?"

"Yes." Patrizia could barely hear her own voice.

The kiss lasted a full minute. Andrea's mouth tasted of tobacco and oranges, and as he pulled away from her, he murmured, almost bitterly, and as if to himself, *"Penso che sia innamorato di te."*

"What does that mean?" she asked softly, genuinely confused, but he had already set off down the street, and she watched as he disappeared into the narrow grid of shops and restaurants.

It was time now.

According to the woman behind the desk at the *pensione,* the Via della Pantera, where Masimilliano Caracci lived, was high up in the mountains above the town, and Patrizia set off along the narrow harbor road until she reached a winding, one-way tarmac road that ascended the mountain. The climb took her forty-five minutes, and when she reached the small, nearly concealed road sign, she was very nearly out of breath.

But everything about her father's property riveted her: the worn white gravel in the driveway, the rusted green mailbox, the olive trees lining the way to the villa, which was medium-sized and the color of ripe peaches, and most of all, the commanding view of the Porto Ercole harbor. At the same time the grounds seemed overgrown and untended, as though the owner had decided to let nature run its course. A small sign hidden in a clump of grass announced, in faded black letters, *I PERAZZI*.

The smell of wild rosemary, mixed with the intoxicating odor of salt air, was almost overpowering. Crossing the driveway, gazing neither left nor right, Patrizia went past the side of her father's villa and onto a sloping lawn. It was here that she set up shop.

Patrizia maneuvered her easel at an angle so that the bright Italian morning light was behind her. Unrolling and then stretching out a canvas, she tacked the sides to the easel with a series of pushpins, before mixing paint onto her palette. These ordinary preparations she could do with her eyes closed, and they took her no more than ten minutes. During that time, Patrizia was alert to any noises or signs of life coming from Masi's villa, but so far, at nine-thirty in the morning, there were none. The only sounds she could hear from this idyllic slope of grass were the sounds of birds calling out, the rustle of the wind through the pine and olive trees, and now and again, the faraway buzz of a motorcycle or a scooter.

Her plan was to paint precisely what she saw: the enormous blue-green mountain off in the distance, and beyond it, the expanse of robin's-egg-blue sky, under which lay the serene Tyrrhenian Sea. A small, razor-hulled sailboat was vanishing around the corner of the hillside, and for the next half hour Patrizia sketched the wind-swollen sail, then moved on to the dark green water.

Three hours later there were still no signs of activity coming from the house. At lunchtime, frustrated that events weren't going according to plan, Patrizia set down her paints and brushes and tentatively approached the front door. The villa was handsome and solid looking, with a grassed-in terrace to one side, some of whose stones, she noticed, were crumbling. Behind the villa, she could make out a pergola, underneath which sat a small glass table and chairs, and behind them, a small circular swimming pool dotted with fallen leaves.

A moment later Patrizia knocked three times—the knocker was a dark brass horseshoe crowned by an ornate fleur-de-lis—and stood there, overcome by a sense of déjà vu. Hadn't she been rehearsing this moment in her mind her whole life? Hadn't she imagined this meeting time and again: the daughter on the front stoop, facing the door, trembling a little, prepared to confront her father, as well as her past—or something like that? In her fantasies, Patrizia was confident, a portrait of calm, but now she noticed that her fingers were trembling.

She knocked repeatedly, but there was no answer. Discouraged, Patrizia collected her things, and reluctantly made her way back down the hillside to her *pensione*.

Back in her room, she began to doubt herself. Was she absolutely certain that the man she'd seen on the street was her father? Could it have been someone who merely looked like Masi? Could she have gotten the name of the town wrong? After all there were many seaside towns with the prefix "Porto," perhaps she had misread the manila envelope at the gallery . . . but no, how many Via della Panteras could there be in Italy? And the man she'd seen casually walking along the street, it *was* Masi.

That night, Patrizia wandered around the narrow, winding streets, hoping to catch sight of her father, but without any luck. Judging from the yachts clustered around the harbor, Porto Ercole clearly attracted a wealthy urban crowd, and feeling out of place, she had dinner at a small pizzeria, then went back to her hotel room. Feeling guilty, at midnight she left a message on Eric's answering machine in New York. "I miss you," she concluded, and it was only when she'd hung up that she realized she hadn't left her number, and that Eric had no way to call her back.

The next morning, Saturday, was bright and windy, and after a small breakfast of cappuccino and *cornetti*, Patrizia started up the hillside again. By now, she knew the route to her father's house by heart: up several stairwells, then hike along the road for fifteen minutes, cut across a small meadow before making her way up the steep hill leading to the Via della Pantera. Exhausted, she turned into her father's white gravel driveway at ten o'clock that morning.

Today, though, she noticed something new: a shiny purple automobile parked at an angle in the driveway. Coming closer, she was able to make out the letters on the back fender: *LANCIA*.

Her heart nearly exploded with excitement.

Still, it was important to keep calm, keep cool. As she'd

done for the past two days, Patrizia set up her canvas on the back lawn, in view of the harbor and the mountains. Stretching out her half-completed canvas, she pinned the edges to the easel, before bringing out her paints, which she proceeded to mix for the next several minutes. Admittedly, though, it was becoming harder and harder to concentrate on her canvas.

Her father had come out of his villa.

Masimilliano Caracci had emerged from his doorway for no reason that Patrizia could see other than to rid the roof of his car of leaves. He was holding an aquamarine-colored dustpan in one hand, a white-bristled brush in the other, and after sweeping the fallen leaves off the path and off the roof of his car, he scraped them into one of the two low green garbage cans that stood at the foot of the driveway.

As Masi was making his way back toward the house, he caught sight of Patrizia. "Hello?" he called out in Italian. When she didn't answer at once, he started toward her. "What are you doing here?" he demanded. Then: "This is private property! You have no right—do I call the police, is that it?"

Patrizia, who had noticed the darkness and surprised anger in Masi's expression, felt, for the first time, frightened. Standing her ground, she stared back at her father, forgetting for a moment that she was Anna Dineen, an American tourist, who had traveled to Italy for one reason only: to paint.

For the first time in her life her father was near enough

to her that she could reach out and touch him. In that moment Patrizia realized that some small, hidden part of her had hoped that he would recognize her. Wasn't that one of her longtime fantasies? That her father would take one look at her and know at once who she was, blood reaching out to blood? But there was no recognition in Masi's eyes, only extreme annoyance.

"Mi dispiace, signore," Patrizia said, sounding as helpless and confused as she could. Then, *"Parla inglese?"*

Masi stopped in his tracks. "Yes," he said, nodding briefly once. "Yes, I do speak English. Who are you? What are you doing on my property?"

To distract him, Patrizia began chattering. "I'm sorry. I was just looking for the best place to paint. There didn't seem to be anybody around, so I took the liberty of climbing the hill and setting up my easel here."

Nervously and unconsciously, she reached up and removed a strand of hair that had fallen in her face and tucked it behind one ear. Masi was still staring at her, assessing the situation. His face was bonier than Patrizia had first thought, with a slightly yellowish cast to it that took her by surprise, but his brown eyes were intense and knowing.

She set down her paintbrush, and hesitantly extended the fingers of one hand. "My name is Anna Dineen. I'm visiting Italy for the first time from the United States." The touch of her father's hand on hers was electrifying, and to disguise her shock, Patrizia apologized again. "I didn't really

know this was anybody's property. I thought . . . well, I
don't know what I thought, I didn't think that anybody
lived here."

"Well, they do. Live here."

"I'm sorry," she repeated, still paralyzed by the proximity to her father.

"Perhaps trespassing on other people's property is permitted where you are from, but here it is is not."

"Mi dispiace, signore," Patrizia repeated.

Masi's manner softened. "You are shaking. Why are you
shaking? Now I am the one who is sorry." He bowed
slightly, formally. "You startled me, that's all. I live alone."
Then, almost flirtatiously: "Is there something about my
face? Why do you keep staring?"

Patrizia quickly looked down. "No reason, signore, *mi
dispiace,"* though to her surprise, Masi no longer appeared to
be listening. Instead, he was looking beyond her shoulder,
at the half-painted canvas propped up against the easel, the
ghostly figures of a sailboat and a mountain. "So," he said
at last, his voice slightly friendlier, "for you, Italy is a good
place for you to paint in?"

The unexpectedness of the question took Patrizia by
surprise, and when she answered, her voice was flustered.
"Well, yes, actually. I mean, it's beautiful, actually. The
whole country is. Especially the view you have here from
your house."

Still studying Patrizia's painting, Masi now took several
steps forward. "So where exactly did you study?"

"I went to art school in the U.S."

"Art school?" Masi repeated the words playfully. "And what do they teach you at American art school?" He didn't wait for her to answer, but instead scanned the canvas with his sharp gaze. "I have never been a huge believer in schools that teach art." Her father's voice was deep, his English stiff and precisely enunciated, as though he had learned it by reading books rather than by speaking. "A school cannot give a student what he or she was born without. In fact, it will merely get in the way of a person living his or her life. Only your life, and what's in it, can give you what you need to paint, wouldn't you agree?"

"Yes," Patrizia said softly. "Anyhow, I'll just pack up and get off your property. Again, I'm sorry that I—"

"Stay."

"I'm sorry?"

"Stay."

"But you live here."

"So? Do whatever you want. I don't have visitors that often, so stay and paint. The view from I Perazzi belongs to everybody. Friends tell me I am a Socialist at heart." Masi turned back toward the house. A moment later Patrizia heard the door slam, and then the house and the property were silent again, and she was aware only of the pine trees and the swirl of traffic from the town below.

For a few minutes she simply stood there, staring at the door to Masi's villa. On the face of it, nothing at all had happened. At the same time she had just met her father. Her *father.* Masimilliano Caracci. She had shaken his hand, felt his solid fingers curl around hers. Little else had taken place between them, no more than a few words, and just like the twenty-two-year-old Lizzie, Patrizia had found herself apologizing over and over again: I'm sorry. *Mi dispiace.* I'm sorry. *Mi dispiace.* Why had she apologized to this man, this man who should have properly been apologizing to her?

Masi's words—their *normality*—had flummoxed her. She had expected an ogre, a monster, someone harsh-voiced, enormous in his impact—not a dark, slender, moody man who'd come outside simply to sweep leaves off the hood of his car.

Idly, as if in slow motion, Patrizia picked up her paint-brush and began mixing colors. It was hard to concentrate on what she was doing, since she was intently aware of the sights and sounds coming from her father's villa—a tele-phone shrilling, a door banging, the whistle of a kettle. Still, she filled in the sailboat, and began sketching one of the hairpin roads that she could see in the foreground, first sketching it with charcoal, then tentatively beginning to mix colors.

Masi did not come out of the house for the rest of the morning. What could he possibly be doing in there? Patrizia wondered. Around noontime, she realized she was hungry. Remembering her promise to meet Andrea for lunch, and their last encounter, she felt suddenly shy and apprehensive. Packing up her belongings, she made her way across the driveway to the doorway of Masi's villa. She knocked on the kitchen door, which opened a moment later, and Masi was standing there, a cell phone to his ear. He looked annoyed. "Now what is it that you want?"

"I was wondering if I could just leave all my stuff here while I go down to the village to get some lunch."

Murmuring something into the phone, Masi finished his call. "I suppose you want a ride down to the village, too?"

"I can walk, thanks," Patrizia said coolly.

"Don't be ridiculous. I will get my shoes."

Inside Masi's maroon Lancia, Patrizia tried to keep her eyes straight ahead, though she found it difficult not to sneak glances at her father behind the wheel. Masi was a fast driver, indifferent to the sharpness of the mountain curves, and also unaware of Patrizia's discomfort. "Where are you going in the village?" he inquired when they were almost at the bottom of the hill. When she told him she was meeting a friend for lunch at her hotel, the *pensione* Monte Cristo, he snorted. "You probably picked the worst hotel in Porto Ercole."

"It was the cheapest," Patrizia said.

For the first time Masi glanced over at her sympathetically. "It's not easy to be an artist, is it?" He didn't wait for her to answer. "Particularly in America. In Italy, art is respected. Why? Because here art has the power to be dangerous. It has the power to incite people. When governments around the world clamp down against their citizens, who do they go after first? The artists, of course. In the States, artists are considered dreamers. *Dopes.*" He seemed proud to know this American idiom, and repeated it. "'Where is the money in art?' they ask." Masi shrugged. "Better to be an artist than a businessperson with a briefcase. They incite nothing in me but boredom."

"If it's okay, I'll come back this afternoon to pick up all my stuff," Patrizia said to him as she was getting out of the car.

Masi waved his hand dismissively. "Whatever you want," and he roared off around the corner.

Patrizia stood staring at the retreating car for a few moments, overcome with confusion, a confusion that she didn't have much time to ponder, since Andrea showed up five minutes later, calling her name excitedly. To her surprise, he kissed her full on the lips. "See? Now I no longer ask you, I just do," he said with a laugh, adding, "I thought it would be more fun to have a picnic outside. So I took the liberty—"

Patrizia took a moment to gaze at Andrea. He hadn't shaved that morning, and his growth of beard gave him an appealingly offhand look that served to emphasize the otherworldly blue of his eyes. When he gestured for her to follow him, she did, along the harbor road and up a stone incline until the two of them reached an overgrown vineyard. "Where are we going?" she asked, but Andrea just smiled.

"You will see."

Striding across the vineyard, Andrea set down the paper bag directly to the left of a yellow flowering gorse bush. "Here is where we will eat," he announced, explaining that they were now atop an old Etruscan fortification that was used during the war with the Spanish. "Look at the view from here," he said. "You can see Elba, and Giglio, and on very, very clear days, you can sometimes be able to make out Corsica."

"How do you know so much about Porto Ercole?" Patrizia asked, but Andrea shrugged. "You will find that most Italians know a lot about their history. It's a small country, Italy," he added. A moment later he opened up the bag.

Patrizia didn't know what she'd been expecting, but it wasn't the lunch Andrea had prepared for the two of them. It looked simple enough: a loaf of peasant bread, a few cloves of garlic, a tub of white mozzarella cheese, several ripe red tomatoes, and a small store-bought cruet of olive oil. Carving the rough loaf—and using his knees as an unofficial chopping block—Andrea poured the oil on the bread, then began chopping large cloves of garlic, which he placed strategically atop the tomatoes, arranging them across the bread, and adorning them with slivers of the mozzarella. "Try," he said eagerly, holding out the first slice to Patrizia, who took it hesitantly, and then, taking her first bite, felt her taste buds explode. Andrea, who was watching her every move while uncapping a small bottle of red wine, looked delighted. "It's somewhat better than McDonald's, right?"

"A lot better," Patrizia said with a laugh.

Andrea handed her a small paper cup of red wine. "I am sorry for these," he said solemnly. "They were all that I had in my car."

Sitting on the hillside, dotted with the yellow gorse and fresh rosemary bushes, with the Mediterranean sun beating down overhead, drinking wine and talking to Andrea, Patrizia lost all sense of time. Two hours later they were both lying on their backs, barefoot, and Andrea was describing his architecture studies at graduate school in Rome. "I think I want to go to the States when I am done," he announced, "and work for a firm there. Maybe start my own business."

"How could anybody want to leave Italy?" Patrizia asked softly.

Shrugging, Andrea smiled broadly. "Italy is not going anyplace."

A moment later he placed his hand firmly on top of Patrizia's. She gazed down at his broad, dark, strong fingers, strangely excited at his touch. "I am so happy to see you again," Andrea said softly. "Do you know how rare it is to meet a girl that you really like? For me, it's rare. I'm—" He shrugged apologetically.

There was a silence. "Picky," Patrizia said shyly at last, "I think is the word."

"Oh, I like that word. That's a good word. Picky, then. I'm *picky*. You teach me a new word, now let me teach you a new word." Andrea thought for a moment. *"La vertigine."*

"What does that mean?"

"The"—and Andrea's hand swirled in the air—"the dizziness?"

"La vertigine," Patrizia repeated.

"La febbre. The fever."

"*La febbre,*" Patrizia said softly.

Abruptly, Patrizia found herself thinking about Eric. At the same time she found herself utterly incapable of taking her eyes off Andrea. Right now it was morning in New York, and Eric would just be waking up, collecting his *New York Times* from the hallway. His waking-up rituals didn't vary much, she recalled. Soon he would shower and shave, sit down at the breakfast table and eat two fried eggs over easy, brush his teeth a second time, then set off on the six-block walk to school. A moment later, as Andrea leaned forward and kissed her lightly on the lips, his lips tasting faintly of wine, all thoughts of Eric left her mind. She knelt forward slightly, meeting Andrea's kiss with an open mouth, and a few minutes later both of them sank back down on the grass, breathing heavily.

"Patrizia," she heard Andrea say after a moment.

She stirred. "Yes?"

"You say that it is your first trip to Italy. Yet your name, you tell me, is Patrizia. How does that happen? You must have Italian blood."

"It's a long story," Patrizia said after a moment. She would have to be very careful. "My father was Italian," she said at last.

"Oh yes? From where?"

"Rome."

"Is he living still?"

"No." For a moment she froze up. "He died before I was born."

"So you have never known your father? What about his family? Do you have any relatives here? Someone you are visiting? Aunts, uncles, grandparents?"

"No," Patrizia said. To cut off this line of questioning, she reached over and put her finger over Andrea's mouth. A moment later she bent down and kissed his lips again, and this time, the kiss lasted longer than the last time. But Patrizia's arm was maneuvered in such a way that she noticed the time on her watch: it was nearly four o'clock. She rose uncertainly to her feet. "Andrea, I have to be getting back."

"Getting back to where?"

"Just . . . getting back."

"Why are you so mysterious?" he asked.

"I'm not mysterious." She was putting on her sandals.

"Yes. You come to Porto Ercole, then you come and go. Now you say you must be getting back. But getting back to what?"

Patrizia didn't answer, but instead continued collecting her things. "What is your rush? What is the hurry?" Andrea demanded. "Did I say or did I do something wrong?"

"It's not you," Patrizia said, aware of the lameness of her reply, but at the same time not wanting to lie to Andrea. She turned to him. "I just have to"—she hesitated—"paint, I told you."

"Paint? You can paint anytime, anywhere, can't you?"

By now, they were back on the main harbor road, heading in the direction of Patrizia's *pensione*. On the docks, men were unloading fresh, dully staring fish from blocks of ice into barrels while the vendors on the waterfront shouted out instructions. "I don't understand," Andrea kept saying. "You and I, we've just—"

"I'll explain another time." Patrizia paused at the entrance to the Monte Cristo *pensione*. "I've had the most beautiful afternoon, Andrea. I want you to know that."

"Have you?" He seemed to be pouting slightly.

Impulsively, Patrizia kissed his lips. "Yes."

"So when do I get to see you again?"

Without thinking, she blurted out, "Tomorrow, I hope," and she started through the front door of the *pensione*.

"When tomorrow?" Andrea called after her. "What time?"

"Dinner."

"Eight o'clock, Patrizia!" he called after her, and as she crossed the small lobby, she caught a final glimpse of Andrea on the sidewalk, gazing through the door at her, looking perplexed.

Back in her small room, Patrizia collapsed onto the small bed. "What in the world am I doing," she said to herself over and over again. It wasn't a question, merely a chain of words she heard herself repeating to herself later as she showered and dressed for her father. Andrea was a complication she hadn't counted on. It made her realize how little she had thought about Eric since she'd arrived in Italy, and this frightened her. Andrea frightened her, too, but for another

reason: for the first time she could remember, she was attracted to a man who excited her. Who made her feel as
though she had no defenses at all.

Or perhaps none of this had anything to do with Andrea
at all. Perhaps it was the August sun that beat down on the
Monte Argentario. Or the red wine that she'd sipped from
a paper cup. Or perhaps it was the sheer strangeness of the
situation in which she now found herself, her identity even
more confused than ever.

To Patrizia's surprise, the sky had begun to cloud over,
and presently it began to rain, the drops light and clipped at
first and then, as the clouds passed over the harbor, intensifying. She waited until the rain had stopped before she
made her way back up the hillside to I Perazzi, though when
she reached Masi's villa, she saw to her surprise that her art
supplies—her paints, her canvas, her portable easel—were
nowhere to be found.

Masi answered the door on the second knock. "Oh,
Anna, it's you. I assume you are looking for your materials.
I brought them inside. You were painting the water, but I
do not think you want your canvas all *covered* with water."
He gazed at her mischievously. "Come in, sit down."

Surprised by his generosity, Patrizia entered the living
room, finding it hard to believe that she was actually inside
her father's house. Here was his furniture—a swayback
chair, an off-white couch with two orange pillows, a bookcase filled with books whose Italian titles she could not com-

prehend. These were his paintings—a bowl of peaches, two sketches of birds, and several ultramodern paintings so primitive looking that they might have been painted by children. Some paintings were hanging, but most were in piles. Patrizia saw to her surprise that Masi had hung her painting against the side of the fireplace.

"So," he said, when she had taken a seat on the couch. "You are trying to paint a sailboat in your picture, right?"

"That's right," Patrizia replied uncertainly.

"Why?"

"Why not?" she blurted out, surprised by the question.

"What is a sailboat anyway?"

"What do you mean, what is a sailboat?"

"I mean what is it? Is a sailboat an animal? Is it a fruit? Is it a vegetable? Is it a kind of weather pattern?"

"A sailboat is a thing," Patrizia replied stubbornly, aware of an anger rising up in her. "It's an object."

"For the person who is not a painter, then of course a sailboat is a *thing,* or an object. That is why you, signorina—"

"Anna," Patrizia said. She cleared her throat. "Anna Dineen."

"That is why you, Anna Dineen, are a painter, and another person—let's call him Joe—is not an artist. To Joe, a sailboat is a thing made out of wood and perhaps—*como si dice?*—fiberglass. The rope is made of a hemp that is hairy when you touch it. The sail is made out of a certain kind of fabric. There is a wheel and seats so your passengers won't complain in rough weather. Now you add to this scene maybe a nice picnic lunch, and you have a sailboat. Right?"

Masi was still gazing intently at her, and for a moment she had to remind herself that she was not his daughter, not Patrizia, but instead somebody named Anna Dineen. "Right," Patrizia said at last.

"But when you are *painting* a sailboat, you are looking at something completely different, am I right?"

"Absolutely," Patrizia said without confidence, not sure she understood what Masi was getting at.

"When you paint, you are not looking at real things, you are looking at *shapes*. You are looking at *colors* and at *mixes of colors*. You are being loyal to what your eye sees, not to what you know to be a fact." Masi's laugh was without warmth, or humor. "When you paint, you must forget about the object that is in front of you. Forget you see a tree, or a house, or a sailboat. Instead, think to yourself, 'Aha! There is a little square of blue. Over there is a little triangle of white. Beyond that is a little oblong color that seems a very nice mixture of pink and brown.' " Masi paused. "And now your job is to paint what you see, just as it looks to you." He shrugged. "My advice to you is to paint what you see, not what you think you ought to see."

"People at art school told me—"

"Oh, never listen to *people*." Masi, she'd noticed, had a habit of sounding bemused, even when he wasn't. "There are too many of them in the world—more and more each year, it seems—and most of them think exactly alike. Listen to the voice inside yourself, Anna." He added, in a kind voice, "Of course, also, if you feel like it, you can listen to me. I do know what I am talking about, you know. When I am not chasing strangers off my property, I work as an art dealer, so—what?—this is your lucky day, as they say."

"You're an art dealer?" Patrizia heard herself say.

"Yes." Masi seemed impatient with this question. "You know, your style is realistic," he said thoughtfully. "You should be doing more representational work. I think this must be a function of something that I can sense is inside you. Some quality of being alone. Am I right? I think impressionists have time and comfort on their hands. They can allow themselves to paint what they don't see. I don't think you are that kind of person. I don't know you at all, but—" He shrugged. "So, Anna—figure out who you are, and you will end up doing the sort of painting that becomes you."

"So how do I figure out who I am?" Patrizia took a deep breath, not really believing that she'd actually asked this question of her father.

Masi had a deep, infectious laugh. "It will all come together in the end. Not to worry. You lack confidence, that's all." He cleared his throat. "Anyway, I am sick to death of talking in my not-very-good English. Anna, are you hungry?"

Patrizia wasn't hungry in the slightest. The meal with Andrea still sat heavily in her stomach, but for some reason, she heard herself say, "Yes. I *am* hungry."

Remembering something. Masi came forward a few steps. "Incidentally, my name is Masimilliano Caracci. Pleasure to make your acquaintance. You can call me Masi."

"Hello, Masi," Patrizia said faintly a moment later.

He bowed gravely, almost mockingly at her. "Anna." Then: "What are you staring at? Do you like what you see?"

Patrizia had been gazing intently at a painting—an off-white canvas with a simple red stripe across it—and now took a few steps backward. "This is one of the most successful painters today in Italy," Masi went on. "What do you see when you look at that painting?"

"Not much," Patrizia said. Then: "It's like a blank wall. It sort of asks you to read into it whatever you want to." She hesitated. "I don't really like art like this."

"I happen to represent the artist."

"Oh, I'm so sorry," she said quickly.

"Don't be. Think for yourself. It is not my cup of tea either, not much modern art is, but"—Masi made a slight noise with his lips—"it is current, and he sells for a lot of money. I like older artists, more traditional paintings myself. Do you cook?" he asked suddenly. Then: "Of course you probably don't. Americans like everything hurry-hurry-hurry. Do you know, for example, how to make a *ragù*?"

"No," Patrizia replied.

"I see I have things to teach you then. Follow me."

A moment later she followed Masi into the large, chaotic kitchen. The aroma coming from the pot on the stove was intoxicating, a mixture of stewing tomatoes and spices.

"It is easy, really." Masi spoke to himself, smoothly, as he stirred the pot. "I hope that one thing you take back with you to America is that there is time, and there is no time. Meaning, we are all going to die, some of us sooner rather than later. But knowing this, we should not rush and forget what we are seeing or tasting or doing. Come here, please." Patrizia felt his arm touch her shoulder, not in an intimate way, but in the way a professor might touch the shoulder of a student to whom he had something extraordinarily important he wanted to teach.

"You start," Masi began, "with one rib of celery, with all of its leaves. One onion. One carrot. Parsley. Sausages, and you want to split these sausages open, take out their meat and with your fingers, you do this—" With his thumb and forefinger, he made a crumbling motion. "Throw away the skins, they are of no use to anybody except the poor sheep whose guts they once held in place. Sometimes I will add a little *prosciutto,* or bacon. Now you add the *conserva.*"

"What's a *conserva*?" Patrizia heard herself asking. She had never been much of a cook—neither had Lizzie— though she had always wanted to learn.

Masi squinted at her, clearly not knowing the proper English translation. "The conserve? The . . . tomatoes that you have reduced. See, you put them"—he reached down under the cabinet and pulled up a copper sieve—"in one of these. And you leave them out in the sun for a few days. Covered, of course." He resumed his lesson. "So we add a cupful of the *conserva* to the onion and the celery and the sausage meat, olive oil, salt, pepper. Then you simmer." He pretended to make a threatening fist. "You do *not* add water. That is my recipe for *ragù*."

As Masi was spooning a small amount of the *ragù* onto bowls of shiny, ribbony pasta, Patrizia wandered around the kitchen. It was clearly the kitchen of a serious cook, with stainless-steel tools hanging from hooks on the sideboard and a variety of large and expensive-looking pans. "How long have you lived here?" she asked presently.

"How long?" Masi squinted again. "First of all, I don't live here. I live in Rome. I was born in Rome and brought up in Rome." He laughed. "It is hard to get me out of Rome, I have to tell you! But in the summers, I like it here, too, because Rome is too hot. Plus, my doctor—" He didn't finish, but added, "Have you been to Rome, ever?"

"Once." This wasn't a lie exactly, but Patrizia didn't tell him that she had been in Rome, and to his art gallery in fact, just the day before. A sudden fear shot through her: had she told Becky her name? Relieved, she remembered that she hadn't.

"Rome is a beautiful city," Masi remarked. "It is a very mysterious city, too—well, this is a very mysterious country, and it can be sinister, too, for tourists. But I like to say that Rome is like an oyster. It hides its pearls from sight. Then all of a sudden you reach in and you find one."

Her father's words froze Patrizia's blood. This was exactly what Sarah said Masi had told Lizzie on another day in Italy twenty-two years earlier. When had it been? Patrizia racked her mind, and then she remembered. It was when Masi showed her mother the Caravaggio painting in the rear of a church somewhere near the Piazza Navona. He had cooked for Lizzie, too, and she had been charmed, just as Patrizia was now. Other scenes from her mother's life crowded into Patrizia's head: Lizzie and Masi riding in his scooter to the restaurant in Rome's Jewish Quarter for fried zucchini blossoms; her mother thinking that she had ruined the painting by Giorno Hals; Lizzie fainting on the sidewalk and waking up later in the hospital. *The world is made up of stairs. There are those who go up and those who go down. If you have this baby, I will never see you or the baby again.*

These last words had the effect of snapping Patrizia out of the reverie she had been in since coming into the kitchen. She turned to say something in response, but by then Masi was holding both bowls of pasta in his hands.

"Do you know that Caravaggio died here in Porto Er-cole?" he asked.

Shocked that he'd brought up the very person she was thinking about, she blurted out, "How did you know I was just thinking about Caravaggio?"

"Were you?" Masi shrugged. "I don't know." He shrugged again. "Maybe you saw his ghost today."

Patrizia searched Masi's face, looking for any indication that he might know, or suspect, her identity, but her father's face was impassive.

"Shall we eat?" Masi asked.

Dinner was served outside on Masi's back terrace, a

comfortable wooden terrace with a millstone for a table and a pergola overhead. There were flowers everywhere, but otherwise the house was sparsely furnished. It was clearly the residence of a man accustomed to living by himself, and Patrizia wasn't sure how she felt about this. On one hand, it seemed to confirm her father's lifelong self-centeredness. Then she suddenly remembered Becky, the woman in the gallery in Rome.

The pasta was delicious—the noodles (which Masi kept referring to as *maccheroni*) cooked perfectly with just the light staining of red-brown *ragù,* the combination of spices and tastes competing with one another for prominence, nothing overwhelming anything else—and so was the lightly dressed salad of greens, the loaf of fresh bread, and the bottle of red table wine. "You are a great cook," Patrizia heard herself saying at one point, and as Masi bowed his head slightly in receipt of the compliment, she privately chastised herself for saying such an inane thing. To her surprise, she was finding it very difficult to hate this man. She was also finding it difficult to keep straight the details of her life.

When Masi asked her where she was from, Patrizia replied, "Chicago." When he asked if her parents were still living there, she replied that her parents were both dead. Patrizia had always disliked lying, but lying in this case was the only way she could accomplish her goal.

"I am sorry," Masi said. Then: "It is difficult to lose both your parents when you are as young as you are. You are how old?"

"I'm twenty-two," Patrizia said. She would be twenty-three in less than a week, a fact she had completely forgotten.

"Fortunately, we do not underestimate the importance of parents in this country," Masi said with unexpected fierceness. "I think of my parents every day. My father, my mother." He laughed lightly. "For better or for worse."

"So how did you become an art dealer?" Patrizia inquired.

"How? I don't know. Lucky, I guess. I always wanted to be around painters. Painting. Since I don't come from much, it was very easy for me to rise up." When he was twenty-five, Masi went on, he'd bought a painting, cheap—"three hundred dollars, U.S."—at an estate sale, and brought it home. "Very simple. Humorous, too. It showed a giraffe hanging from its neck over a chair. It was not signed by any artist. What does this mean, a giraffe hanging from its neck, right? Two months later I get a call from the lawyer from the estate. They tell me they made a mistake and now they want to buy the painting back from me. And they offer"— Masi did the calculations in his head—"one thousand dollars, U.S. I hang up the phone. Two days later they call me again." This time, the lawyer offered five thousand dollars, and again, Masi said no. "By now, I figure this painting has to be something good, right? I take it to an expert. He tells me it's a Magritte, a gift, maybe, to the lady whose estate it was. Never before seen." Every couple of weeks, Masi continued, the lawyer called, offering higher and higher sums for the return of the painting. "By now, I of course know the painting is extremely valuable. But Magritte or not, it is also a *thing*. An *object*. So when the figure reached four hundred thousand, U.S."—he shrugged—"well, maybe I am weak, I said yes. With the money, I opened up my own small gallery. And"—he paused—"it turned out I am rather good at it."

"I suppose you had a lot of time to devote yourself to your work," Patrizia heard herself saying. "Without a family or anything." Then, more boldly: "So were you ever married?"

"Married? Me? No. Do you see a ring on this finger? And why do you ask?"

Patrizia felt suddenly uncomfortable, and she tried to keep her voice light. "No reason."

"I hate to disappoint you, my dear Anna. You are an extremely attractive girl, but I'm old enough to be your father." Masi laughed. "Also, I am what you call in America a 'bad bet.'"

Patrizia didn't understand at first—and then in a flash, she did. She had never felt quite so embarrassed in her life. "That isn't what I meant," she said, flustered, but he cut her off.

"I enjoy your company, Anna." Masi's voice was kind. "How old are you again?"

"I'm twenty-two."

"Literally—I have a child your age."

The words came from nowhere, and hearing them, Patrizia felt herself going a little faint. She leaned back against the back of her chair, and the cool wicker managed briefly to steady her nerves. She was aware only of the expectant silence in the room. Did Masi suspect her? Was he simply playing along? If he knew that she, Patrizia, was his daughter, this would certainly be the right time to say something. Instead, he gazed out at the dark lawn, and beyond it the crescent-shaped harbor. "Twenty-two years old," Masi repeated softly, as if there were nobody else in the room.

"Where does your daughter live?" Patrizia asked softly.

Masi's gaze snapped back to her. "Did I tell you I had a daughter? I said a child."

"No," she said hurriedly, embarrassed. "I don't know why, I just assumed—"

Patrizia found the blankness in Masi's eyes chilling. It was as though he'd extinguished a part of himself. "It was a good guess," he said suddenly, harshly. "It's one of those things. Like you, she lives in America." He stood, a sudden agitation in his manner. "The mother wants nothing at all to do with me. I cannot say I blame her—well, who knows—but human curiosity being what it is—" He didn't finish the thought, and instead turned to Patrizia. "What else may I get you? Another espresso? Some cheese?"

Patrizia watched as Masi collected the plates, then vanished into the kitchen. She rose and followed him, unsure of her own motives.

"How old did you say your daughter was?"

Masi's back was to her, his elbows moving as he rinsed the plates and bowls and stacked them inside the dishwasher.

"Your age. Twenty-two." He made a strange whistling sound with his lips. "It is strange, though, to think back on when *I* was was twenty-two. Back then I thought I knew all there was to know about this life. In fact, the twenty-two-year-old boy—so full of himself, so guided but also *misguided*—he knew nothing. I look at him now, and I want to—you know—strangle him sometimes."

"Why?" Patrizia heard herself asking.

Masi didn't seem to have heard her. "But that is how it works, you know? You look back and sometimes you cannot even recognize that person that you were."

"What did you think you knew everything about when you were twenty-two?" but just then, Masi was interrupted by the telephone ringing. "Another time," he murmured before picking up the phone. *"Pronto,"* Patrizia heard him say.

She could not understand what the conversation, which was conducted entirely in Italian, was about. All she knew was that she had a glimpse of her father as he must have appeared to Lizzie that final afternoon in the Piazza Navona. The veins stood out on his forehead; and his brown eyes appeared to turn a scary black. By the end of the conversation, he was shouting at the person on the other end of the line. When Masi hung up, he tried to contain his anger, but it was nearly impossible. "I cannot believe this!" he kept saying. "Five weeks away, and he does this to me!"

"Does what to you?" Patrizia asked. She felt suddenly

uncomfortable, as though she didn't belong in the room. "Who did what?"

"In five weeks I have an exhibit, right? At my gallery? All the press, the newspapers, all my friends come to this gallery opening. A collection of paintings by young artists. Now one of my artists has decided to go on vacation with his girlfriend to Geneva, Switzerland, of all places. There is no painting. He calls me from the road." And now he imitated the artist. " 'Masi, I'm so happy, I'm so in love, I can't paint when I'm happy.' "

"Can I paint you a picture?"

Patrizia's own words shocked her. She was aware only of her father's dark, shrewd eyes, and behind him, the still-running faucet, and the gleaming copper pans. "Never mind," she added quickly. "Thank you very, very much for dinner," and she started for the hallway.

"*Dilo di nuovo*. Sorry—say what you just said again."

"I didn't say anything," Patrizia said. "I just said can I try painting a picture for your exhibit." Feeling strangely panicked, she glanced around her for her jacket but couldn't find it, and instead reached for something she thought was her jacket, but which turned out to be the arm of her sweater.

Masi had followed her into the hallway. "You want to paint something for me? For my show? Is that what you are asking?"

It was next to impossible to read the expression in her

father's eyes. Was he mocking her? Was he patronizing her? And why, and how, had those words come out of her mouth?

"How fast are you?" Masi inquired suddenly.

Patrizia's expression showed she didn't understand the question.

"I say: How fast can you paint?" Masi repeated.

"It depends," Patrizia replied, taken aback.

"And what does it depend on? Time? Money? Inspiration?"

"Time, I guess."

"Three weeks."

"Three weeks what?"

"Can you finish in three weeks?"

"I don't know if I could—"

"I am not saying I would take it. You know that. But I am—" Masi didn't finish his thought. "Money is a problem for you, too, am I right about this? I assume you are not staying in the worst hotel in Porto Ercole because it gives you pleasure, right?" Embarrassed, Patrizia nodded. "That would not be a problem. There is a guest house out in back I let some of my artists use if they are well behaved. Right now it's empty. You are welcome to it." The studio had a single bedroom, he went on, as well as a bathroom, a small kitchen, and best of all a studio. Because of its location halfway down the hill, it was quiet and private. "You are welcome to stay there." He stared at her challengingly. "What do you have to say?"

For a moment Patrizia couldn't respond. She was aware of a strange, unfamiliar battle going on inside of her. "Why do you trust me?" she heard herself asking.

"Why?" Masi shrugged. "Who says I trust you? But I am a realist. And if you turn out to be a bad person, or a bad artist, which I doubt"—he laughed his mirthless laugh—"then I will simply ask you to leave."

"I'll have to go back down to the hotel and get my things."

"I'll drive you and wait outside."

"No, I mean—" Patrizia was embarrassed. "I'm actually having dinner with somebody. A guy," she added.

Was she imagining it, or did a look of disappointment cross Masi's face? "A secret life?" he said. "Ah, no. I will not ask you that."

Five minutes later they were racing down the mountain in the purple Lancia. Masi drove quickly and seemed pre-occupied, and after dropping Patrizia off in front of the *pensione* Monte Cristo, he said only, *"Le vedrò domani.* Until tomorrow."

As she stood there on the sidewalk, Patrizia felt strangely divided between her father and Andrea. The thought made her laugh—it was as if she'd re-created a typical dilemma from the life of a typical American daughter. Wasn't this exactly what she had planned? Still, this notion gave her no pleasure, and her mood only worsened during dinner. Andrea seemed sullen and argumentative, particularly when Patrizia gave him only a sketchy account of her day. "I painted Andrea, what else am I supposed to tell you?" she asked.

Andrea laid down his silverware and gazed darkly at her. "Again, you give me these answers that are not answers, really! What is it all about?"

"Just my natural female mystery," Patrizia replied, trying to turn the question into a joke. "Me and Mata Hari."

"Sometimes I think you are running away from me. Or else you are some kind of secret person."

Patrizia gazed back at Andrea, wanting to tell him the truth about what she was doing in Porto Ercole, the truth about her name, the truth about her father. But something told her this would only disappoint him, that it might sabotage what had happened already between them. Instead, she placed her hand gently on his hand. "What was it you said to me the other day? In Italian?" she asked softly.

"I can't remember."

"It was something like *sia innamorato*. Something like that."

"I can't remember," Andrea repeated. Then: "Go look it up in one of your Italian guidebooks."

Still Patrizia parted from him on good terms, agreeing to meet again for dinner the next night, a plan that seemed to cheer Andrea up. "I think I am bored and a little bit restless," he said before he left. "I have nothing to do here except wait to see you again. *Penso che sia innamorato di te,*" he blurted out suddenly.

"There, you just said it again!"

"Because it is such a strange thing for me, that's why!"

"What is?"

"The fact that I think I am falling in love with you!"

Patrizia gazed at him, astonished. "Me, too," she said suddenly. She came forward and kissed him, very lightly, on the lips. Despite herself, her voice came out a rushed murmur. "Good night, Andrea."

After breakfast the next morning, Patrizia collected her clothes and checked out of the *pensione*. Twenty minutes later she was in the backseat of a taxi heading up the mountainside to her father's house on the Via della Pantera. Masi had left her a key to the guest house, and now Patrizia unlocked the door and let herself in, unpacking her clothes on the small mattress in the back. Now, recalling the conversation she'd had with her father when he was dropping her off at her *pensione* the night before, she felt as confused as she'd felt in a long time.

"I can speak plainly to you. You are quite talented," Masi had said as they made their way into the dark, deserted Porto Ercole village. "I would not waste my time with you, frankly, if you were not." He was silent. "I must say I am sorry for your sake that you are talented."

"You're sorry?" Patrizia blurted out without thinking.

"Better to be mediocre. Easier and less frustrating, wouldn't you say?"

Patrizia felt at a complete loss for words. From the moment she first laid eyes on Masi, she had been overcome by her own vulnerability. In the face of that vulnerability, her anger had receded almost completely, and she'd attempted to regain her authority. But she couldn't. Instead of being repelled by him, she'd found herself entranced by his attentiveness. He'd noticed when her glass was empty, or when she had finished her bread. He'd asked her about herself, about her impressions of Italy, about what kind of art she preferred, and who her favorite artists were. He'd discussed American and Italian history. Don't fall for this, Patrizia ordered herself sternly at one point. This is exactly what he did to my mother, asked her lots of questions, made her feel as though she were the only person in his world, the most interesting, the most beautiful . . . "What about Renoir?" Masi had asked her at one point during dinner.

"I love Renoir," Patrizia said. She had inherited Lizzie's love of the artist, his colors and his sensuality.

"I think it's that you remind me a little of someone I knew a long time ago. She was also an American. She very much loved the paintings of Renoir, too."

Then there were other times when Patrizia had caught Masi gazing out the window, or else staring at his own hands, lost in a reverie, and the expression in his eyes at those times was so melancholy and difficult to read that it frightened her. Once he noticed her staring, and made a wan attempt to smile. "You must forgive me. I find I have been very tired recently. I think it is simply that the older I get, the less I can deal with the hot weather."

As Patrizia unpacked her clothes, she could see out the window: on one side, her father's villa, a radiant peach under

the midday sky, and on the other side, a group of day fishermen puttering out on primitive motorboats across the glis-
tening water. She loved everything about I Perazzi—the
house, the pergola, the smells, the breezes, and most of all,
the view of the harbor. Never in her life had she stayed in
such a beautiful place. It was shaping up to be a beautiful
day, too, with a stiff breeze that carried with it a faint tang
of fresh rosemary.

5

∞

Awakening early the next morning, Patrizia arranged her easel outside on the back lawn in preparation for her first day's real work. Remembering Masi's warning that Porto Ercole suffered from occasional water shortages, and that the municipal office tended to shut down the town supply during the morning hours without warning, she made certain that she had several cupfuls of tap water for mixing paints before beginning.

She had never felt so nervous in her life. It was as if all the painting she'd done so far in her life had simply been a dress rehearsal for the task that now lay before her. The actual subject of her painting was simple: the Porto Ercole harbor. The Tyrrhenian Sea, with its constantly shifting colors. A winding road, a passing sailboat, a few clouds overhead in funny, drifting shapes. But what about the composition of the picture? Was it any good? Or should she scrap what she'd done so far, and start over again?

A few minutes later, unable to concentrate, Patrizia set aside her paintbrushes, her mind helplessly focused instead on the two men who had come into her life: Masi and Andrea.

Too much had happened much too quickly, she reflected. What was the matter with her? Wasn't this exactly what she had planned and hoped for? To get close to her father for the purpose, somehow, of injuring him, betraying him? For the purpose of hurting Masi as badly as he'd once hurt her mother? As badly as Masi's absence had affected herself, ever since she was old enough to understand she didn't have a father in her life? Had she forgotten why she had come to Italy in the first place?

But her plan, vague in the extreme, had been completely upset by the sight and the sound and the touch of Masimilliano Caracci. So far, Patrizia had found that by the sheer force of his personality, Masi was the one who seemed to be controlling her, not the other way around. Even though she had presented herself to him as a stranger, she could see through to his kindness and his warmth, and even to his hospitality. As well as hints of those qualities that Lizzie, according to Sarah Bogan, had also noticed: his stubbornness, his flashes of anger, his controlling nature.

Yet when Masi had complimented Patrizia on her painting, she had responded in a way that had taken her completely by surprise. Rather than wanting to hurt her father, she found instead that she wanted him to be proud of her. She had walked into his life intending to overturn it, and instead, she'd discovered how much she still needed from him twenty-two years after he had walked away from her mother in the Piazza Navona. How had it happened that Masi, with a few offhand words of encouragement—*you are quite talented; you are an extremely attractive girl*—had managed somehow to alter the way she looked at herself?

It wasn't that other people hadn't encouraged her during her lifetime. Patrizia's teachers in art school were forever praising her technical skills and her use of color. The Chicago gallery owner who had mounted a series of her paintings in a Michigan Avenue coffee shop told Patrizia he had received so many compliments for the show that he would extend the exhibition for another month. Then there was Lizzie.

When Lizzie was alive, there had always been a faint element of competition between mother and daughter, though Patrizia had never felt altogether comfortable admitting this to herself. When a seventeen-year-old Patrizia had told Lizzie of her ambitions to become an artist, Lizzie had replied, coolly, "Well, a lot of people want to grow up to be artists," though later she apologized for not embracing her daughter's ambitions more wholeheartedly. When Patrizia moved to New York, Lizzie told her on the phone one night that she was returning to painting herself. "Maybe someday somebody will exhibit *my* work," she told Patrizia, and Patrizia had hung up on the phone feeling as though she'd somehow offended her mother.

Or was it simply now that in retrospect, Patrizia was able to imagine how complicated it must have been for Lizzie to have a daughter who was an artist? Lizzie, who as a teenager had pored over the lives of great artists and learned by heart the colors of Renoir's palette, Lizzie, who in her early twenties had wanted to be an artist herself. Sometimes Patrizia wondered how her mother had felt about giving up her passions—first art, and then art conservation. How had she felt about heading off every day to a job that barely tapped her abilities? A job that had comically little to do with what she did best? Did Lizzie accept that this was how her life had turned out, or did she regret the missed chances, the vanished opportunities?

Patrizia remembered how sometimes, in the mornings, when Lizzie was just waking up, her voice would be husky and girlish, and she would laugh in a way that was unfamiliar to Patrizia. It was a voice and a laugh that made her feel as though she didn't know her mother at all. It was as though the person Lizzie had presented to her daughter on a daily basis was in fact only a familiar role, a comfortable identity. And that the real Lizzie, the one who showed up flickeringly in laughs and in morning voices, the Lizzie who was young and headstrong and artistic and a little wild, was somewhere else, perhaps back in Italy, perhaps bent over a table, polishing a painting alone, thinking about Masi.

It wasn't that there hadn't been men in her life. There

was Ron, with his beard and bow ties and professorial manner. There was Peter, stooped and slightly boring, as well as several other suitors over the years. But Lizzie hadn't been head over heels in love with any of these men, and as she'd told Patrizia more than once, "I'd rather be by myself than be in a relationship that doesn't excite me."

Early that morning, Masi had arrived at the door of the guest house bearing a tray with several jugs of bottled water, "in case you get thirsty during the night," he explained. He wandered through the small house, checking to see if everything was in order, and satisfied, he motioned for Patrizia to take a seat on the living-room couch. "You may wonder why I am allowing you to use my little house," he said, his expression serious. "And you may wonder to yourself, Who is this man? Would he allow anybody he met to just move into a guest cottage on his property? Has he completely lost his marbles?" This American expression seemed to please him, and Masi chuckled. "The answer is no. But perhaps we can both do each other a favor here."

"What kind of favor?"

"Well, if your work is good enough, who knows?"

There was a silence. "Who knows what?" Patrizia asked, but Masi didn't answer the question. "If there is anything you need, please let me know."

"I can get whatever I need in the village later—" but the impatient look on Masi's face cut her short.

"You are my guest," he said crisply. "I will provide whatever you need." As he was leaving, Masi informed Patrizia that he'd been called away to Rome unexpectedly, and would be back late the following afternoon. "I apologize there is no car for you here," adding that there was an old bicycle in the garage. "I checked it this morning," he said. "The tires are"—and he held his thumb and index finger in a circle—"perfect."

It wasn't only Masi who dominated Patrizia's thoughts, it was Andrea. Andrea: just saying his name, to herself or aloud, gave her a strange, almost illicit pleasure. She hadn't forgotten that she would be meeting him for dinner that night at the *pensione* Monte Cristo. When Masi was gone, Patrizia labored over what to wear, finally deciding on a simple black dress that showed off her dark eyes. By seven that evening, she had worked herself into such a state of excitement and apprehension that on her way down the hill toward town, she was nearly cut down by a speeding sports car.

Inspired by Andrea, Patrizia had bought a small Italian phrasebook in the village, feeling that it wasn't fair for Andrea to have to shoulder the entire burden of communication. She now knew the Italian words for bowl (*la scodella*), dinner plate (*il piatto*), napkin (*il tovagliolo*), and table (*il tavolo*). Well, if nothing else, it was a start, and it would make Andrea happy.

Descending into Porto Ercole, Patrizia made her way down a winding side street to the entrance of the *pensione* Monte Cristo. There she leaned against the side of the building, checking her watch: she had at least a half hour before

Andrea showed up. She was about to head off to the magazine store to browse the newspapers and magazines when Andrea suddenly emerged from the lobby of the *pensione,* with a furious expression on his face.

"Andrea—" Patrizia called out, and he turned.

"I don't know what you're doing, Patrizia," he said angrily. "But it's a lie, isn't it?"

"What's a lie?" she said, aware of a sudden dip in her stomach.

Andrea spoke in rapid Italian, as if to himself, his voice so emphatic that it attracted the attention of several pedestrians on the sidewalk. Finally bits of English broke through. "I go to your *pensione,* and what do they tell me? They tell me you have not been there for two days now. That Patrizia Orman, she has moved out. So what am I to think?"

"Andrea, I'm not staying at the Monte Cristo anymore," she said desperately. A wave of anxiety filled her stomach. How could she have been so idiotic as to have agreed to meet him in front of the *pensione*? How could she explain to Andrea that she was now staying in the guest house of a villa high above the harbor, when she had told him quite plainly that she knew nobody in Porto Ercole, or for that matter, in all of Italy?

"Why? Why do you check out? Why do you tell me you are going to meet me here? Do you not want to meet me after all, is that it?"

Gazing at his face, Patrizia saw that Andrea was less upset by the fact that she was no longer staying at the *pensione* than by the notion that he would not see her ever again. "Andrea, I've been thinking about you all day," she said softly, relieved.

"Oh, this I doubt—"

"I have. Andrea, I can explain." Though what, and how much, was she going to say, exactly?

"Are you who you say you are? Is your name Patrizia?"

"Yes—"

"So where are you staying now? Where do you sleep?"

"I'll explain everything to you at dinner," she promised.

"Dinner, well—" Andrea paused dramatically, still confused and angry, and took a moment to light a cigarette, inhale, and exhale in a long, trembling funnel. "I don't know about dinner with someone who *tricks* me. Who tries to *fool* me."

"I wasn't trying to trick you or fool you," Patrizia said lamely, and a moment later she grasped Andrea's hand, a gesture that seemed to calm him down a little bit. "And so what was I going to think?" he demanded as they walked toward the center of the town. "One day you're here, the next day you're not. So what was I going to think? Maybe you have run away from me?"

"I would never run away from you."

"Yes, but how would I know that?"

"Because," Patrizia said, "I learned the word *napkin* for you." In spite of herself, she burst out laughing. It was the first time she'd laughed in a long time, not since her

mother's death, and for some reason, she found herself unable to stop.

Andrea looked on, pleased and embarrassed. "I think
you are crazy," she heard him say affectionately. "What do
you mean you learned 'napkin' for me?"

"Napkin," Patrizia said, still gasping with laughter. "*Il
tovagliolo*. Right?"

"And so what?" Andrea pretended to look insulted.
"Am I a napkin? Are you calling me a napkin?"

"*Il tavolo*," Patrizia gasped out.

"And now you are calling me a table. This is not good,
any of this. I am a man, not a table or a napkin—" though
by now, despite himself, he was starting to laugh, too.

"Why these words?" he kept asking as they entered the
restaurant. "I am glad of course you know the word now
for 'napkin,' but you should learn other words as well."

"Like what?"

Andrea didn't answer, since a waiter was now leading
them to a small table in the back of the restaurant, which
was long and narrow and crowded, with blue-and-white-
checked tablecloths. *"Un tovagliolo, per favore,"* Patrizia said
to the waiter as soon as she was seated, and the perplexed
expression on the waiter's face made her burst into giggles
again.

"Okay, now you tell me," Andrea said when their
steaming plates of *linguine alle vongole* and *tortellini con prosciutto* arrived at the table. "And please, no more silly talk

about napkins. I am proud of you for learning, but first I want you to explain things to me."

Patrizia hated not telling Andrea the whole truth, but she felt she didn't have any choice. "I met an art dealer," she heard herself say at last, feeling torn. "He lives in the hills, in a villa called I Perazzi—"

As Patrizia went on to explain that the art dealer had taken an interest in her painting, and offered her the use of his guest house, she noticed that Andrea was becoming agitated again. "And what's this man's name?" he demanded.

"Masimilliano Caracci."

"Sure." Andrea's shrug was casual. "I know that name."

Patrizia's stomach dropped. "How?"

"Famous dealer of modern art. Very well known, well respected. He has a gallery in Rome, right, if it's the same guy? So why are you looking at me so surprised?"

Patrizia was shocked that Andrea knew her father by reputation. "I just thought what with Rome being such a big place—"

"I keep telling you Italy is not so big a place. And so anyway, what does this guy Caracci want with you?"

When Patrizia told him that she was attempting to paint a portrait for a gallery opening several weeks away, Andrea gazed across the table at her with new respect. "Congratulations," he said quietly. "That is quite an honor."

"Well, he might not like it—"

"That he even asked you," Andrea replied. "Ninety-nine percent of artists in Italy would love to be in your place right now." He was silent. "So does this guy, this Caracci, does he like you?"

The question took Patrizia by surprise. "He's been very encouraging," she started to say.

"You don't understand. I mean does he *like* you. The way that I like you."

Patrizia thought back to the moment of misunderstanding in the living room of Masi's house, when he'd been under the impression she was flirting with him. She had never felt so horribly embarrassed, and the memory brought back a sudden color to her cheeks. "Andrea, don't be ridiculous."

"Well, how else am I supposed to react? You tell me that you are staying at the house of an older man, what am I supposed to think?"

"In a guest house," Patrizia reminded him, "where all I do is *paint*."

Andrea made a dismissive gesture with his hand. "The guest house is probably near to *his* house, right?"

"I swear to you, Andrea, it's not like that."

"I understand. Of course I do. What would you want with someone like me anyway?"

Patrizia met his searching gaze with her own. *"Penso che sia innamorato di te,"* she said gently.

Andrea didn't understand. "Now you imitate me!"

"I'm not imitating you. I'm saying it. I mean it."

Patrizia realized to her shock that this was true, and fearful of her own words, she finished her meal in near silence, achingly aware that Andrea was gazing intently at her. "What?" she asked several times, and every time, he replied simply, "I love looking at your face, that's all."

"Andrea?" Patrizia asked softly, boldly, as they were leaving the restaurant. "What do you think will happen?"

"Will happen what? You mean between you and Caracci?"

"No, I mean—"

"Between you and me, you mean?" Andrea was silent. "I don't know. I know what I *want* to happen." His cheeks had reddened. "Come," he said suddenly. "We go, okay?"

They made their way along the harbor road, pausing to admire the shimmering lights of a yacht berthed at the harbor, passing well-to-do Italians out for an after-dinner stroll, or perched at tables in small coffee shops, talking animatedly over cigarettes and cups of coffee. Past a shuttered row of fish-vending stalls, the road became residential, and as she and Andrea passed a cluster of condominiums, Patrizia was aware all of a sudden of the stars and the large fuzzy moon, the sweet odor of rosemary mixed with the not altogether unpleasant smell of fish. Andrea clasped her hand in his. "Shall we go up on the hill to see the view?"

At the top, they found an old wooden bench, and for the next several minutes they sat gazing at the silent beauty in front of them, and not saying a word: the dim bow lights of a yacht cruising majestically through the harbor, the spot-lit staircase across the harbor ascending to the centuries-old Etruscan fortifications, the lights of villas concealed in the mountains. When Andrea reached over to kiss her, Patrizia's lips responded, but when his fingers moved toward the buttons of her shirt, she gently pulled away. "What's going on?" Andrea murmured, as if in a trance.

"We can't here."

"We can't what?"

"You know what I mean."

"So where, then? Please? I want to be with you."

A moment later Patrizia held out her hand to him. "Come with me."

"Come with you to where? My car?"

"Just come with me, that's all."

Up the winding hillside. Across the slender tarmac road, hand in hand, alert to sounds of any oncoming traffic. The trees, so familiar to Patrizia during the daylight, now seemed as though they were connected by a single dark trunk. Neither Andrea nor Patrizia said anything as they made their way across the long, pebbled driveway of I Perazzi, past Masi's villa with its lone driveway light cocked to one side and on to the guest house, Patrizia's key jamming slightly in the lock, Andrea managing finally to open the door. And then the two of them were on Patrizia's small bed, their lips locked together, fumbling for each other's zippers, buttons, clasps.

Briefly, guilty, Patrizia couldn't help but flash back to Eric, whose friendly but slightly mechanical lovemaking always gave her satisfaction, but not much else. For some reason, she pictured Eric in his pajamas, brushing his teeth, then spitting out the toothpaste into the sink. Andrea's touch was different, lighter, more skilled than Eric's, and it electrified her. Their bodies were a precise fit, and Patrizia found herself hating the fact of skin, both hers and Andrea's, and how it kept them apart. Afterward, vaguely ashamed of her own passion, she found herself inching away from him. "It's so hot," she heard herself say, hating the falseness in her voice.

"Hey," Andrea called out softly. "Patrizia, where are you going? Come back here." He found his discarded pants on the floor, and brought out a pack of cigarettes. "For you?"

Hesitantly, Patrizia allowed Andrea to light her one. She'd never been a smoker, but smoking in Italy felt different. Though where had she heard that before? Someone who hadn't smoked before she had come to Italy, but who had adopted the habit to avoid feeling left out?

A moment later Patrizia realized: it was her mother.

She stubbed out her cigarette, and made a face. "Yuck. It's too hot in here to smoke."

"Are you sure this is okay, you and me being here?" Andrea asked after a moment.

"I'm sure," Patrizia said, trying to sound confident, though not really feeling that way. She felt guilty about bringing Andrea back to the guest house. It was almost as though she were an adolescent sneaking her boyfriend into the house while her parents were away. Though come to think of it, wasn't that precisely what she had done?

"How do you know Signore Caracci is not here?"

Patrizia explained that Signore Caracci—she was careful not to call him "Masi," which implied familiarity—had gone to Rome, and would not be returning until tomorrow afternoon. "Andrea?" she asked softly.

He turned so he was facing her, his index finger lightly stroking her bare hip. *"Sì."*

"Do you know at the restaurant when I asked you what was going to happen, and you said you knew what you wanted to have happen? What did you mean by that?"

Andrea was silent. "I meant," he said at last, "I meant that I wanted to be with you. All the time." He gave an incredulous laugh. "This never happens to me, you know? Liking somebody this much? Feeling as though it was supposed to be this way? Feeling as though I've met the person I was supposed to meet? I mean, *my God!*" Again, the incredulous laugh. "I could see myself wanting to get married to you! For me, it's that bad!"

"Bad?"

Andrea's voice softened. "Good is what I mean, of course."

Patrizia wanted to tell him that she felt the same way. That she could see herself sharing a life with him, that she could see herself . . . and then a cold wave of fear passed through her. Andrea was now lying on his back, gently fanning himself with one of her drawing tablets. "I have an idea," she said suddenly.

Baked all day by the hot Italian sun, Masi's small swimming pool was so warm it felt almost slick on Patrizia's skin.

There were no pool lights, so she and Andrea swam in the darkness, the warmth of the tiles against their feet, and then Andrea came up behind her, cupping her breasts in his hands, and covering the back of her neck with kisses. "Stop," Patrizia said, giggling, and Andrea was saying, "You want me to stop because you like it," when her attention was riveted, suddenly, to the sound of a car pulling into the driveway.

"Oh my God—" she whispered to Andrea. "We have to get out."

A car door slammed, and now Patrizia heard footsteps. By now, she was out of the pool, naked and dripping wet, searching desperately for a shirt, pants, anything, with Andrea behind her. "What did I do with my clothes?" she whispered, panicked. She pictured them, suddenly, on the floor of the bedroom in the guest house, next to Andrea's hastily discarded jeans; she hadn't even brought out a towel, and neither had he. Ducking down for no good reason, and indicating that Andrea should follow her, Patrizia started toward the guest house, and when they were back inside, she collapsed onto the bed, relieved, her heart still pounding. From the window, she could see the purple Lancia parked at an angle in the driveway. What was Masi doing back from Rome so soon? More to the point, had he seen them, or heard their voices?

Patrizia waited there, on the bed, for a long time, until Andrea, who was looking slightly stone-faced, said, "I think it's okay now. The lights in his house, they just turned off."

"You have to leave," she whispered, and nodding, Andrea dressed quickly, in silence.

"When will I get to see you next?" he whispered. Up close he smelled of salt water mixed with sweet, an odor Patrizia found herself breathing in deeply.

"Tomorrow's not good," she whispered.

"The next day, then."

"The day after tomorrow, then." Why had she told him that tomorrow wasn't good? Patrizia had no plans that she knew of. Instead she repeated, "The day after tomorrow, then."

It was nearly ten o'clock the next morning when Patrizia again picked up her paintbrush. She had spent a fitful night, dozing and awakening again and again, dreaming vividly of Andrea. She couldn't remember the details of what she'd dreamed, merely that it had involved an encounter between him and Masi, and that Masi had chased Andrea off his property with a weapon of some kind—a shovel, or a broom. Awakened by the chattering of birds, she'd gotten up late, prepared herself a cup of coffee, and watched the sun rise over the Porto Ercole harbor. After a second cup of coffee and a light breakfast of *cornetti,* Patrizia went though every room of the guest house, searching for any evidence that Andrea might have left behind. Afterward, satisfied that he hadn't left anything, she set up her easel outside on the lawn. Still, aware of Masi's presence in his villa, she found it difficult to concentrate, even more so when Masi appeared suddenly from behind the house. *"Buongiorno,"* he called out. "And how is my artist friend this morning?"

"I'm fine," Patrizia replied as brightly as she could, for some reason finding it difficult to look him in the eye. Then: "I didn't expect you back from Rome so soon."

Masi shrugged. "Schedules change."

They chatted for a few minutes, Patrizia still avoiding his gaze. Yes, Rome had been sweltering. Did Anna know, Masi went on, that so many merchants left Rome in the summertime that several years back the government had had to step in and demand that a certain number of shops and supermarkets remain open in August? Still, he liked the heat. "I find it pleasant," adding that it reminded him of his childhood in Fiumicino. Suddenly Masi inquired, "Anna—are you a smoker?"

The question took Patrizia completely by surprise. "No," she managed to say. "I mean, sometimes in a weak moment—"

Masi held out his hand. There were three or four curled cigarette butts in his palm, and Patrizia's heart sank: they were Andrea's, and perhaps one of hers. "And so perhaps you had a few weak moments yesterday," he said.

"I'm sorry," Patrizia started to say.

"Or perhaps they belong to your friend in the swimming pool?"

When Patrizia glanced up at Masi, to her surprise she

saw that there was no anger in his face at all, only amusement. "I can explain—" she started to say.

"What is there to explain? Personally, I am happy that you have found someone to be close to. People think love is easy, that it happens all the time. Well, it doesn't." Masi took a few steps closer. "So this boy—is he good to you?"

"Yes," Patrizia said softly, unable to face the truth of the matter, that Masi had probably caught a glimpse of her and Andrea in the swimming pool the night before.

"And is he Italian? Did you meet him here?"

"Yes." Patrizia could barely hear her own voice.

"Because if he is not good to you, well then, you must tell me." Masi laughed without humor. "Be careful, okay?"

"Okay," Patrizia said, oddly touched by his words. Then: "I'm really sorry I brought him here. It's just"—she faltered—"well, we didn't have any other place to go."

Masi made a dismissive gesture with his hand. "Do you think I care that you brought a boy here? Please. What you do is your own business. I just don't want you to smoke, that's all."

"I'm sorry—"

"Morally, I couldn't care less, of course. But it is a terrible habit, and it will kill you. Do you promise me that?"

Patrizia was puzzled by the remark. Without asking, she had brought a young man back to her father's guest house. They had made love, swum in Masi's pool, and the only thing Masi was worried about was smoking? Taken aback, she nodded. "I promise you."

"Good. Now—take a little walk with me, will you?"

For the next few minutes Patrizia and her father made their way down the hill in silence until they reached the paved road. On the other side was an ancient banister that led down to the water, and Masi slowly made his way down the stairs, with Patrizia following close behind. Stepping behind the railing, Masi motioned for her to do the same. Hesitantly, she ducked underneath the railing and followed him along a winding path that led to a small overgrown field dense with wildflowers.

Masi made his way across the field, pausing every now and again to stoop down and pick up a scrap of garbage, or a rock, or an odd-shaped stick. From the field, the view of the water was an iridescent blue, and Masi took a seat on a boulder, gesturing for Patrizia to sit beside him.

The two of them stared out at the blue-green Mediterranean water for a long time. The day was already hot, and the sardine smell that Patrizia had noticed earlier seemed to have intensified in the heat. When she commented on it, Masi informed her that there was a sardine-canning factory near where they were sitting. "Can you feel the sirocco coming?" he asked suddenly.

Masi explained that a sirocco was the name of a Mediterranean wind that made its presence known in Italy in the summertime. "Terrible," he said. "Humid, gusty, it makes your sinuses feel like they want to explode, and you feel like you want to murder someone." He glanced out at the water again. "Do you know, this is one of my favorite spots in Porto Ercole. My father grew up here, you know. Then his family could not afford to live here anymore." Masi was silent. "It was here, at his request, that I scattered his ashes."

Masi's father. That meant Patrizia's grandfather. Patrizia knew nothing about Masi's family, even though they were her family, too. "Were you close to your father?" she heard herself asking.

"It depends, I guess, what you mean by close."

"What was your father like?"

Masi frowned for a moment. "Like everybody, he had his good sides and his bad sides," he said. "He worked hard for our family. But I saw him practically never. Weekends, sometimes." He shrugged. "Why, what was your father like? Were you and he close?"

Taken aback by the question, Patrizia's thoughts spun in her head. "I didn't see much of my father, either," she replied hurriedly. "So, no, I wouldn't say that we were close."

"You are like me, then."

Patrizia gazed at him in disbelief. "I guess so," she said softly at last. "I guess I am like you in that way."

"Everybody needs their father," Masi remarked thoughtfully. "No matter how old they are. We all need somebody to tell us we are doing all right, and that we are making the right choices. We all need to be told that we can accomplish anything. I miss him." He was silent for a few moments, and then he sighed heavily. "How is the painting going?"

"It's going all right," Patrizia said. "I haven't really had time to—"

"Then you must *create* the time. Are you serious about this or not?" Masi's voice had suddenly turned harsh. "If you're not serious about your work, then you are wasting my time and yours."

Patrizia gazed back at him, shocked. Still, she managed to blurt out, "I *am* serious."

"Good. I thought so. So why do you waste your time going for a walk with me? Next time I ask you to come with me, I want you to say back to me, very politely, 'No, Masi, you are a wonderful, interesting, charming companion, but I have work that I must do instead.' And I will miss your company, but I will also understand. You see." He squinted. "Anna, shall we walk down to the water?"

"Sure," Patrizia said, without thinking.

"Have you heard nothing I just said? Let me repeat: Anna, shall we take a walk down to the water?"

Patrizia gazed at him evenly. "Masi, you are a wonderful, interesting, charming companion, but I have work I have to go do instead."

"Good. Now go do it."

It was a dismissal. Patrizia rose awkwardly to her feet. "So I guess I'll see you back at the house," she said lightly, but Masi gave no indication that he had heard her. Making her way back up the stairwell, she turned to see her father still gazing out at the water, his legs crossed, his fingers linked behind his head. A small part of her felt like turning back, and retaking her place beside him. She sensed a strange loneliness in Masi today, and felt he needed companionship. But in the end she turned on her heels and made her way back to the guest house.

∞

Never before in Patrizia's life—not in college, not in art school, and certainly not on her own—had she worked so hard.

Over the next week and a half she understood finally what it meant to commit herself to her art, though at first she found herself resisting. Why should she spend every single moment of her day painting? What about having a life—going for a swim, taking a nap, reading a book, or spending the afternoon with Andrea? But another side of her knew Masi was right: that if she was serious about her work, then she would have to prove it.

Her desire was very simple: to create an extraordinary painting for her father. And to make him proud of her. Patrizia was aware, as well, of her own feelings of vengeance. Three weeks ago, she reflected, she had wanted to destroy her father—to hurt him, to betray him, to do precisely to him what he'd done to Lizzie twenty-two years earlier. Now this desire was replaced by another desire: she wanted to destroy her father with her talent, her eye, her technique, her commitment—and finally, with a finished painting he loved.

At first, Patrizia chafed at the limits Masi had imposed on her time. The day after their walk, he had appeared at the door of the guest house, and asked to look at what she had painted so far. Reluctantly, she brought him into the studio where her painting sat tilted against an easel. Masi gazed at it for a long time without saying anything, then finally he cleared his throat. "Sloppy. You can do better," he added languidly. "I suggest you change your schedule."

It wasn't a question—to Patrizia, it felt more like an order. "You sleep too late," he went on.

"I do?"

"Yes. That is no good. Half the day is done by the time you start work. I want you to begin early in the morning. Mornings are best. Why?" Masi answered his own question. "Because not only are you the most energetic, but you are closest to the time that you sleep and you dream. For you, I suspect that your dreaming time is one of the few times you allow yourself the freedom that you need in your painting. Do I make any sense?"

Of course, every single one of his artists was different, Masi went on, but on the whole, most worked from the time they awoke until two in the afternoon, then resumed after lunch and a nap until nightfall. "This will work for you, too. Try it tomorrow."

Patrizia was surprised by her own boldness. "I do have a life, you know," she heard herself saying.

"You mean the boy? Of course, go see your friend. Solitude loses some of its meaning unless it serves as a refuge from other people. Plus, I think the boy is good for you."

"You don't even know him."

"True. But you have changed since you arrived here. Probably the boy, what's his name—"

"Andrea," Patrizia said softly.

"Probably Andrea had something to do with this, wouldn't you say?"

"What's that supposed to mean?"

"Oh—" Her father raised his hand as if to scratch his forehead, but instead, brought his hand back down again to his side. "Forget I said anything."

"I'd be happy to," Patrizia replied, and to her surprise, Masi laughed uproariously.

"Now you know what a sirocco is like. You hate me today, right? A sirocco makes everybody hate everybody else."

Sirocco or not, Patrizia had found it surprisingly easy to create a schedule out of the hot, formless days of the Porto Ercole summer. She awoke early, at five-thirty or six o'clock in the morning, first preparing herself a thermos of black coffee, then dragging her easel out onto the lawn to begin work. Though she hated to admit it, Masi was right: the discipline of her new routine not only benefited her work, it made the prospect of seeing Andrea all the more enticing.

It had taken Patrizia some time to convince Andrea that even though she no longer had as much free time as before, she still cherished the time that they spent together. He took her for drives around the Argentario Peninsula, exploring the small villages and port towns surrounding Porto Ercole. One day, as a surprise, Patrizia rented a small sailboat, and she and Andrea spent an afternoon lazing on a sandy, isolated beach accessible only by water. More and more, though, Andrea seemed to be in a funk, and when she asked him what was wrong, he told her he was thinking ahead to architecture classes resuming in the fall. "What are your plans?" he asked her one afternoon. "Will you be staying on in Porto Ercole, or will you come back with me to Rome?"

Patrizia didn't know the answer to his question. A great deal depended on whether or not Masi liked her painting. But she realized that this was just a smoke screen, one that failed to take Andrea into consideration. Andrea, who had become more important to her than any painting, more important than any gallery opening, more important than, well, just about anything. "All I know is that I want to be with you," she told him.

"I love you, Patrizia," Andrea said in a quiet voice. It was the first time he'd ever told her that, and stunned, Patrizia could only stare at him. "Me, too," she said quickly, then told him she had to hurry back to I Perazzi to finish her painting.

∞

The preparations surrounding his upcoming exhibit had exhausted Masi. He came around to the guest house far less than he once did, and he spent an increasing amount of time talking on the phone. He looked drawn, and pale, and despite what he'd told Patrizia about his love of summer, and heat, she noticed that her father spent most of his time in the air-conditioned rooms of his villa, and that he avoided eating his meals outside under the pergola. Several times, she was surprised to hear him coughing, long, rattling coughs audible from the guest house, that typically lasted for five minutes or more.

The first time she offered to cook him dinner, Masi naturally refused. "You are a guest in my house," he told her firmly, but two days later, at the end of an afternoon in which Patrizia had overheard him shouting at someone on the phone for over an hour, her father took her up on her offer.

Patrizia was scared to cook for him, but to her surprise, he seemed to enjoy the meal she'd prepared: a baked risotto with chard and bacon, a salad of chicory, arugula, and walnuts, and a fresh loaf of peasant bread. Later, over small cups of espresso, Masi turned to her very suddenly. "I think it is not so bad a thing for me to have you here, Anna."

The remark seemed to have come out of nowhere, though his voice was strangely melancholy. "What do you mean?" Patrizia asked, feeling a shiver of apprehension pass through her.

"I mean that you are giving me an opportunity—the only one I will ever have probably—to be—" but then Masi dismissed his own thought. "No," he finished.

Patrizia persisted. "No what?"

"I don't know." Masi was silent. "You see, you are the age of my daughter." Again, he hesitated. "And so maybe I am able to give a little to you what I should have given to her all these years. I don't know—does it work that way?" An edge had crept into his voice. "See, I have sent various things here and there to my daughter, but I suspect her mother does not give them to her."

"Who was the mother?" Patrizia heard herself asking, but Masi didn't seem to have heard the question. Instead he fell silent again, then changed the subject. Some nights, she had noticed, Masi's English was better than it was on other nights. Tonight was one of those evenings when she was reminded that everything her father was saying came through a veil of translation, and she could have kicked herself for not having made more of an effort to learn Italian.

A few nights later, however, as they were eating an informal lunch in the kitchen, he turned to her. "You asked me a question the other night that I did not answer. You asked me who the mother of my child is." Without waiting for Patrizia to respond, Masi added, "She was a beautiful American girl. An art conservator. Very gifted at what she did. Once I was very much in love with her. Her name was Elizabeth. I called her 'Li,' which is—how do you say it?—a nickname."

"Li," Patrizia repeated, her heart beginning to pound in her chest.

"Li was very—" Masi laughed suddenly. "I think it is

very hard sometimes for an Italian man to deal with a woman like that."

"Like what?" Aware that she had accidentally snapped at him, Patrizia repeated the question, this time more softly, though Masi hadn't seemed to notice.

"An independent woman. A woman who knew what she wanted. I don't know . . ."

When he didn't continue, she asked softly, "So what happened?"

"She got pregnant. By me, of course, though I accused her of other men. I was not ready to settle down and have children. Like many men, I wanted first to make my mark in the world before I brought a child into that world. I said terrible things to her. I loved her, but—" Masi shrugged. "We were two people at different stages of our life, that's all. I am not proud of that fact, but there it is, a fact. I will not love a woman like that again, ever. And I will not forgive myself for that." He cleared his throat. "You will find that most Italians are realists. But back then, now I don't know who the realist was, whether it was me, or Li."

Remembering her father's behavior toward her mother, Patrizia felt a fleeting distaste for the man in front of her, a distaste that vanished when Masi added, "As I said the other night, though, perhaps I can give to you, Anna, some of what a father is supposed to give to a child he has never met."

"What do you think a father gives to a child?" Patrizia heard herself asking shyly.

"Well, I would say it depends completely on the child, right? A girl is so different from a boy."

Patrizia took a deep breath. "Let's say it's a girl."

Masi thought for a moment. "I think I don't know the answer to that question you ask. I will have to think about it a little." His voice became suddenly brisk. "Anyway, Anna, I thank you for appearing in my life at this time when I find myself thinking about the past so much, and with such"—he paused—"complicated feelings here and there."

For a few minutes Patrizia could not move from her seat. Tears had sprung to her eyes, and she turned away so that Masi wouldn't notice them, but he did anyway. "Did I just say something terrible to you, Anna?" he asked kindly.

Patrizia excused herself to clear the table. In the kitchen, she ran the hot water until the sink was full, then submerged the plates and bowls and glasses. Alone, her tears came faster, especially when she realized that she'd just witnessed the closest thing to an apology that she would probably ever hear from her father's lips.

When she returned to the living room, to her surprise Masi had fallen asleep, his head flung back against the pillow, his breathing labored. Noticing how chilly the air-conditioned room was, Patrizia grasped the small red-and-blue-checked throw blanket that lay on top of the couch, and arranged it gently across her father's unmoving body, tucking it carefully around the edges so that it wouldn't fall off if he stirred in his sleep. "Sleep well, Daddy," she whispered almost inaudibly, so that even if Masi had been awakened, he wouldn't have been able to make out what she was saying.

∞

The next morning it took Patrizia an hour or two to realize that it was her birthday. The fact of it surprised her: she'd given this day practically no thought, and nobody, not even Andrea, knew that today she was twenty-three years old. "Happy birthday, you," she said to herself in the mirror. She considered taking a day off from work—perhaps calling Andrea and arranging to meet him in town for lunch, perhaps heading down to the dock with him, renting another boat, and puttering around the bay in search of more isolated beaches. Then she remembered that in her present circumstances, August 31 meant one thing only: Masi's gallery opening was in exactly three weeks, and feeling a faint wave of panic in her stomach, Patrizia set to work finishing her painting.

She started off by adding a slight bit of paint to the sail of the sailboat, though dissatisfied by the tilt of its bow, she sanded it down before reapplying a thick second coat of paint. A few dabs here, a detail there. Now Patrizia concentrated her attention on the boat's hull. She had never achieved the precise color that she wanted—so why not mix up paints she'd never mixed before? Why not try something new, and if that didn't work, then she could try something else?

Patrizia had never felt quite this way before—so willing

to take risks, so unconfined—and for the next ten hours she painted in an uninterrupted frenzy, not even noticing that lunchtime had come and gone, or three hours later, that shadows were beginning to streak the lawn. By five o'clock that afternoon, the painting Patrizia had now completed bore scant resemblance to the painting that she had been working on for the past two weeks. The sailboat now resembled nothing so much as a pattern of white triangles, suggesting speed, acuity, sharpness—but certainly not a sailboat; and as for the water, she had scraped away everything that she'd done, and instead painted the Tyrrhenian as her eye saw it: a turbulent mass of blue gray with stretches of vaporous pink that dissolved into the late-afternoon summer sky.

Two hours later, when Patrizia finally laid down her paintbrush, she felt exhausted, frightened, and proud. It was done. Her painting was finished. She was tempted to go back and clean up a few small details, but a remark Masi had made about one of his more nonproductive painters, who spent a year or more on each painting, drifted through her mind. She decided to leave the painting alone, and take her chances.

When Masi answered the door, there was Patrizia, her hands and arms speckled with paint. "I'm done!" she exclaimed, her own excitement surprising her. It was obvious she was disturbing her father—his face was slightly puffy, and as he brushed past her, she could smell traces of alcohol on him—but noticing her exultant expression, he said slowly, "We'll go have a look, then."

Patrizia felt suddenly foolish, and frightened, and worried. Was Masi all right? Granted, she hadn't known him for long, but in that time she had never known him to drink more than two glasses of wine. Tonight, however, judging from his unsteady gait as he made his way across the lawn, he had clearly exceeded that amount. Moreover, what if he hated her work? As Masi joined her by the door to the guest house, she had a moment's awful doubt—maybe she should go back and work on the painting a little more. "Now, you probably won't like what I've done—" she started to say, and Masi responded with a crooked smile.

"Please, Anna. I think I can make up my own mind."

As Masi stopped short a few feet away from the easel, Patrizia hung near the door as if to make a quick escape if her father's reaction was negative. Masi moved in closer, then took a few steps backward. A moment later he opened his mouth as if to say something, then closed it again, before turning to her. His bright eyes revealed nothing. When he held out his hand, hesitantly, Patrizia took it. Masi's fingers closed over hers, and their two hands stayed that way for a few minutes, with neither one of them saying anything. Releasing her hand, Masi turned with a smile toward the door. "I knew you could do it," he said simply. "Good work, Anna."

Was that all he was going to say? For a moment Patrizia

stood frozen in place, then she called out to his retreating figure, "Thank you!"

Masi was halfway back to his house, and now he stopped and turned, the same lopsided smile on his face. "Thank me for what? Everything you needed was always inside yourself. You did it. If you thank anybody, it must be yourself." He resumed his slow, unsteady walk back toward the house.

The following day, however, Masi was a new person—restless, energetic, and full of plans. "I have made arrangements for you to stay at the apartment of a friend who is away from Rome until December," he informed Patrizia as they were leaving Porto Ercole. "It is in the neighborhood of Trastevere, which I think you will like. The apartment is yours for the month of September, and afterward, we can discuss more paintings, more exhibitions, and the future." He was silent for a moment. "There is much ahead of you, Anna," he said quietly. "You are one of those painters—and I suspect one of those people—who can accomplish whatever it is you set your mind to."

Andrea had wanted Patrizia to drive back to Rome with him. "Why do you want to go with Caracci?" he asked. When she explained to him that she felt she owed it to her host, he pouted. Finally they reached a compromise. Andrea would drive several cars behind them "just in case Signore Caracci tries any funny business with you." He added, "Patrizia, I cannot *wait* to show you Rome."

Patrizia stared sadly at the window as the Lancia left the Monte Argentario, and turned onto the highway south, heading toward Rome. She had no idea if she would ever return to I Perazzi, but a small voice inside her told her that it was unlikely. Masi noticed her gazing out the window. "Every summer, it is harder and harder for me to leave. And this summer, most especially."

Patrizia glanced over, expecting him to say more, but instead, he reached down to turn up the volume on the air conditioner. "We must all concentrate on the present, not the past." Masi smiled. "Too cold for you?"

"It's fine."

"Incidentally—I must apologize for last night."

"What about last night?" Patrizia asked, though she knew exactly what he was talking about.

Masi was staring straight ahead, his eyes well hidden behind dark glasses. "I was not really prepared for your visit, for your finishing your painting. Yesterday was my child's birthday. I take that day usually to indulge in a little self-pity. Very sentimental, and not a very smart habit, if I say so myself." He cleared his throat. "I drink to my child. Then I drink too much." He fell silent.

Only a few times during her brief visit to I Perazzi had Patrizia been tempted to divulge her identity to her father. The day she first laid eyes on him, and again, during their first meeting there, when Masi had taken her hand in his. But never since then, not even once. Now, however, she was overcome by a powerful impulse to tell him everything:

about herself, about Lizzie, about all she knew. *Yesterday was my birthday, too,* she would start off. *What a coincidence, eh?* Then she would watch Masi's expression of astonishment as he put two and two together.

But her father's mind was already on other things. "The usual people will be there," Masi was saying. "We expect many people for opening night, and many more in the weeks that will follow." The paintings would be set up in no particular order, he went on, with one important exception: Patrizia's painting would be the first painting that visitors saw when they came into the gallery.

Patrizia couldn't believe this. *"Mine?"*

Masi turned to her. "Of course yours. You don't get it, do you?" he went on kindly. "You don't realize how good you are, do you? I actually find it is one of your most charming qualities."

The Trastevere section of Rome where Patrizia was staying was an arty neighborhood that many visitors likened to New York's Greenwich Village. And there *were* similarities: the narrow, crooked streets, the multitude of restaurants and sidewalk cafés, the festive, fashionable atmosphere. The apartment that she would call home for the next month was colossal—six high-ceilinged rooms, exquisitely furnished, and overlooking the Ponte Sisto. Before giving Patrizia the key, Masi handed her a white business-sized envelope. "A small advance on your work," he said. "And please don't think I'm being generous. I will be getting all of it back, and more, after the opening."

When he was gone, Patrizia opened the envelope, and pulled out a check. The figure shocked her: eighteen million lire, which came to approximately ten thousand dollars—by far the largest single amount she had ever earned for a painting in her life. She set the money aside in a drawer, relieved. She had been down to her last two hundred American dollars, and was wondering how she would make ends meet. Now she no longer had to worry.

With her painting finished, Patrizia was free to see as much of Andrea as she wanted, though now that he was back in school, his schedule was unexpectedly tight. To Patrizia, this came as a mixed blessing. It was true that she'd been busy herself in August, but now that she had free time on her hands, she realized she'd been using her painting as an excuse to avoid seeing Andrea. The reality of this confused her. She was in love with Andrea; that much was obvious to her. Why then, increasingly, did she find herself avoiding him? Why did she find it so much easier—and safer—to communicate with him on the telephone? In his presence, she felt increasingly tongue-tied and agitated, and whenever he asked her what was wrong, Patrizia would come up with an excuse that rang false even to her own ears.

Still, despite her apprehensions, she and Andrea made it a point to meet two or three times a week, usually in Trastevere, which Andrea knew well. On one of their meetings, they spent the afternoon touring medieval churches: Santa Maria dei Sette Dolori, designed by Borromini, as well as Patrizia's favorite, Santa Maria in Trastevere, with its twelfth-century mosaics by Cavallini. Afterward, they returned to Patrizia's apartment, where they made love for hours, Andrea lighting up a cigarette afterward, and Patrizia declining, remembering her promise to Masi. The following week, Andrea took her to the Casa della Fornarina, a well-known restaurant, as well as the final home of Margherita, the baker's daughter, who had served as the model for Raphael's famous portrait *La Donna Velata*—The Woman with a Veil. On the way back to her apartment, Andrea handed her a small, paper-wrapped cone that he'd bought from a street vendor. "It's called *grattachecca,*" he announced. "It's ice mixed with a kind of syrup. It's the best thing in the world, you have to try."

Without thinking, Patrizia blurted out, "I don't want it."

Andrea gazed at her, confused. "Well, thank you very much, Andrea." He looked wounded. "What is the matter with you, Patrizia?"

Food. The tastes and flavors of Italy. The still-stagnant heat of September in Rome. A handsome young man taking a young woman to his city's local attractions, offering her Roman specialties, looking on proudly as the woman tasted a spoonful. Trastevere, where the offices of a trustworthy abortionist were located. "I have to go, Andrea," Patrizia said hurriedly, and when she reached her apartment, she found to her surprise and increasing agitation that there was a message from Masi on her answering machine.

Since they had come back from Porto Ercole, Patrizia

had seen little of her father. Scrambling to get his show ready in time for opening night, which was less than two days away, he had been largely out of touch, though now and again he would leave a friendly, rambling message on Patrizia's answering machine. Tonight, his message was more pointed than usual: two buyers, one Swiss and the other Italian, had made simultaneous offers on Anna's painting, and Masi wanted to meet with her in order to discuss the terms. He knew it was late notice, but would Anna please join him for lunch tomorrow at a small restaurant near the Campo dei Fiori?

The next day, when Patrizia showed up at the trattoria, she was surprised to see that Masi was not alone. Nearing the table, she saw to her dismay that the woman from the art gallery, Becky, was seated to his left, and that the two of them were engaged in intimate conversation. When Patrizia appeared at the table, Masi leaped to his feet. "Anna! This is Becky, she is a friend of mine, also from America—"

As Becky shook Patrizia's hand, she stared at her strangely. "Don't I know you from—" she started to say, but Masi interrupted her.

"This is Anna, the one I've been telling you about." Briefly, he related the story of how Patrizia had shown up one morning at his Porto Ercole house "like a street urchin," acting as though the entire country of Italy was her landscape. "Well, it turned out to be my lucky day," Masi said with a laugh, adding, "and I hope Anna feels the same."

"That's quite a story," Becky said when he was finished

talking. Still, she seemed confused, and it was only when Masi excused himself for a moment to talk to a friend across the room that she gazed across the table at Patrizia. "Well, congratulations," she said. "A lot of people really love the painting you did."

"Thanks," Patrizia said, avoiding Becky's gaze.

There was a silence. "So," Becky said. "It looks like you're quite the operator."

"What do you mean?"

"Oh please." Becky's smile was thin. "You just *happened* to show up at Masi's house in Porto Ercole, saying you were a painter? What an incredible coincidence."

"It's not what you think," Patrizia started to say, feeling hopelessly confused.

"I thought you told me Masi was a friend of your mother's."

"He *is* a friend of my mother's—"

"And you just happen to be an artist who wanted to get your work exhibited." When Patrizia started to respond, Becky cut her off. "No, really. In a perverse way, I admire people like you. You get exactly what you want."

Patrizia understood suddenly: Becky was jealous of her. As far as she was concerned, Patrizia was a competitor for Masi's affections. Despite herself, Patrizia laughed. "Really, it's not at all what you think." She couldn't resist adding, "I'm young enough to be his daughter."

"And that's supposed to make me not worried? You're funny." Becky smiled serenely across the table. "Actually, he and I are planning on getting married next year, so actually I don't care what you do."

The news came as a shock to Patrizia. During the month in Porto Ercole, Masi had mentioned nothing at all about Becky. Married? It seemed unlikely, and she was relieved when Masi returned to the table. "Are you two getting acquainted?" he asked. "That's good." To Patrizia, he added, "Becky is my girl Friday. She keeps my life sane."

All during the lunch Patrizia was unable to concentrate on what Masi was saying, and instead found herself sneaking glances at Becky and at her father, observing the interaction between them. "I think the price he offered is fair," Masi was saying at one point. "You don't want to overvalue a beginner's work, or buyers resent you." He turned to Patrizia. "Did you ever give your painting a name?" When she shook her head, he said, "Well, we must think of one. I like to avoid *Untitled* as much as possible."

She didn't know how she lasted through lunch. As the three of them were leaving the restaurant, Masi informed Becky that he would drop her off at the gallery, then proceeded to give her a long list of things he needed done that afternoon. As she was exiting the car, Becky shot Patrizia a poisonous look. "So where are you two going anyway?" she asked Masi casually.

"I am going to show Anna a very special part of Rome."

Patrizia had never seen gardens quite so magnificent as these of the Vatican. The grass was a lush green she'd rarely seen before, and the trellises and the flower beds were a riot of magnificent color—reds, purples, oranges, yellows. Later she could have sworn she had seen colors that did not exist—combinations of purple and lime, of yellow and ocher. "I am fortunate to have access to the Vatican Gardens," Masi remarked as they made their way along one of the paths. "One of the big shots at the Vatican—no, not the pope, I promise—is an artist in his spare time. Several years ago I agreed to represent his work. In return, he gave me clearance to use these gardens. I find them to be perhaps the most serene place in all of Rome. I come here sometimes just to think, just to be alone."

Masi paused in front of a magnificent line of olive trees. "Anna, it has been such a joy getting to know you. It has been a privilege to be in your life." When Patrizia blushed, he added, "I mean that! You can go anywhere you want to go. You can do anything you want to do."

"Thank you," Patrizia said softly. For a few minutes they walked in silence across the immaculate lawns, and finally she screwed up the courage to ask the question. "So who's Becky?" Her voice sounded hollow.

"Becky? Oh, she works with me at the gallery."

"Really?"

Masi gave her a quick glance. "Really."

"Are you really planning on marrying her?"

He gazed at Patrizia almost disappointedly. "And who said that?"

"She did. Becky did."

"Did she? What an interesting thing for her to say."

"Is it true?"

"No. It is not true." Masi shrugged. "Sure, yes, we talked about all this, but I find this is something many women like to talk about. Society may change, but the earliest dream for so many women remains the image of themselves in a white wedding dress, strewing petals left and right." He pantomimed the scattering of flowers. "*Ahh. Ohhh. Ahh.* So corny," he added. "Becky is a dreamer. She is also very uptight. She believes, I think, that Italian men can free something stuck in her. It is the Latin-lover cliché, and it is only that, a cliché." Masi paused on the path. "So, no, in answer to your question. I am not going to marry anybody. I have, of course, a larger reason against marriage, but I will not go into that right now." He gave his strangely harsh laugh. "She is good fun, Becky. I like American women. They know how to have fun."

I know, Patrizia felt like saying, *until you grow tired of them.* Instead, she heard herself saying, "So you're not getting married?"

"Of course not. That would not be fair to her or to me. Next question?"

"You mean you're just going to dump her?"

"That is a hideous way to phrase it. No, there is no need to dump her. For the time being I enjoy Becky's company."

Patrizia pictured Becky's face then. She was just a girl from—where had she said she was from? Buffalo? Vermont? Some small, rigid, northeastern state. She had found her way to Italy, where she'd met a middle-aged man, no doubt a refreshing change from the American men she had known all her life. A man who had probably bowled her over with his cultured, educated mind, his charm, his humor, the intensity of his gaze. A man who could talk at length about wine, food, opera, soccer, politics, history, theater, mathematics, art, and artists. Inevitably, she had fallen in love with him. But soon—and Becky didn't know this part yet—it would be over.

An ancient fury that Patrizia thought she'd put aside rose up in her chest again. It felt strange to feel this way in perhaps the most peaceful spot in all Rome, the Vatican Gardens, a place devoted to contemplation and serenity, but as she made her way toward the gate, she was aware that her breathing had tightened and her walk had quickened. "Anna, what is the matter?" Masi asked. "Is there something wrong?"

Patrizia whirled around. "Wrong? Why would there be anything wrong?"

He stared at her for a moment, and then his face relaxed into a smile. "You have the bad nerves before the opening. If I were you, I should go home and rest."

"I don't need to rest."

"Anna—"

"That's *not* my name."

Patrizia couldn't believe she'd said it, finally, and for a moment she regretted having opened her mouth. But by now it was too late.

"What do you mean?" Masi came closer. He gave a little laugh. "Wait, don't tell me—now that you are a successful artist, you are going to change your name to—let me see, what could we name you—"

"Do you know that my mother came to Rome when she was my age, too?"

Masi looked more indifferent than surprised. "You never mentioned that, no. So . . ." Now he seemed to be at a loss for words. "And so, did she enjoy herself in our fair city?"

"Absolutely. She loved it here, in fact. Do you know what her favorite place in Rome was?"

Masi was gazing at her, puzzled. "How would I know that?"

"The Piazza Navona."

Masi shrugged. "The Piazza Navona is a beautiful place. Why not have that be a tourist's favorite place? I can think of worse places. But, Anna, why are we talking now about your mother?"

"I told you, that's *not* my name," Patrizia repeated loudly.

"And what is your name?"

She ignored the question. "My mother was twenty-two when she first came here. Just like me, she wanted to be an artist. But she was also working as an art conservator—"

"Oh."

"—at the Istituto del Restauro."

As she was speaking, Masi's expression had grown very still.

"She fell in love," Patrizia went on. "I mean, Rome is a pretty easy city to fall in love in, so she did. She met this wonderful, handsome, interesting Italian man. He was a student at the Giuliocesare at the time, but he was full of plans. And just like any woman, my mother listened to him. For instance, someday he wanted to open up his own art gallery—"

"You must stop," Masi whispered.

"And someday he would drive the car he had always admired. It was called a Lancia. Someday the two of them would get married and have children. They couldn't really decide on what to name the baby if it was a boy, but they agreed that if it was a girl, they'd name her Patrizia. Oh, and wait—here was another plan that the guy had: someday he'd be enough of a big shot in his profession to be able to walk freely through the Vatican Gardens, maybe because he thought that walking there might confer on him a certain class, a certain set of values that were otherwise missing in his life—"

"You are . . ." Masi didn't finish. "I cannot believe—"

"Then, when this American girl found herself pregnant—oh, her name was Lizzie, by the way, but the Italian guy, he called her 'Li' for short—she went to the only person who could really understand her. The Italian guy—"

"Is that what I am to you?" Masi interrupted softly. " 'The Italian guy'?"

"And what did he tell her? He told her that if she had the child, then he would never see her again."

"I told you—"

"And here's the best part: he'd never see the child again either. I mean, we're talking real Father of the Year material here."

"Patrizia—"

"Oh, and here: then he reached into his bag of sayings and came out with this one: *'Il mundo è fatto a scale; c'e chi scende e c'e chi sale.'* Did I say that right, *Dad*? Is that good Italian, *Dad*?"

"Yes," Masi said very softly. Then: "It *is* good Italian. I would expect nothing less from my daughter." He muttered something rapidly in his native language that Patrizia didn't understand, before breaking back into English. "Patrizia—that is your name, right?"

"Yes—"

"Patrizia, come here—" But she wheeled away from his outstretched hand.

"Do you have any idea what it was like growing up without a father?" Her voice rose. "To be in my mother's position, raising a kid all by herself, with no money? Do you know what Mom ended up doing? Taking the first miserable job she could get. Working as a *secretary* at a university just so she could afford to pay for her kid to go to art school. Cutting corners, clipping coupons—"

"I sent her many checks—"

"So maybe she didn't want to cash them, isn't that unbelievable? Why would she want your filthy money? Believe it or not, we didn't want your money, we wanted *you*."

"I tried to provide—"

"We were *poor*, Masi. Do you have any idea what it's like to be poor?"

"As a matter of fact, yes, I do—"

"No vacations, Mom driving the the same piece-of-crap car her whole life that ended up killing her."

"What do you mean, that ended up killing her?" Masi froze in place.

Tears were falling down Patrizia's face now. "Yes!" she shouted. "Lizzie's dead! She was killed in a car accident six months ago! My mother's dead, she's gone, and you'll never see her again! And neither will I!"

Masi had turned away from her, his shoulders heaving, and then abruptly he turned back to her, his voice steady. "Understand something—"

"There's nothing to understand. I understand *everything*."

"You are a very beautiful girl," he said suddenly.

"Stop!" Patrizia brought her hands to her ears.

"You look like the two of us. I can see both of us, right now, in your face."

"I don't care!" she shouted, her voice ringing out across the quiet gardens. "It's too late! The world is made of stairs, and you, Masi, are on the bottom! I guess some things never change." Patrizia was backing away from her father now. "I'm glad I got a chance to know you, *Pop*," she called out.

A pigeon wheeled out suddenly from behind a bush, momentarily startling her. "But unfortunately, you are exactly the same person that you've always been and that you always will be. And frankly, I just feel sorry for you."

Patrizia ran, leaving behind her father, who was standing in the garden, calling out her name over and over again. Across the broad piazza of St. Peter's, and then she was hailing a cab to take her back to Trastevere. The cabdriver glanced curiously at the tears falling down her cheeks but said nothing. Back at her apartment, she packed frantically, hurriedly, carelessly stuffing her art supplies and portable easel into one bag, her clothes into another, her passport and her wallet, stuffed with the money Masi had advanced her for her painting, in the inside pocket of her coat. Looking around her, she checked to see if she had forgotten anything. No. It was as though she'd never been in Italy in the first place, never been there in her life. Then, on a whim, Patrizia pressed the button on the answering machine.

There were three calls, all of them from Andrea. "I must see you tonight," the first message said. "It's very important." The second message was a repeat of the first, and the last message said simply, plaintively, "Call me. Please." Then: "I love you."

Patrizia didn't call him back. The only call she made was to a car service to take her to Leonardo da Vinci International Airport.

6

∞

Gazing skyward, Patrizia stood behind the middle-aged Italian couple as they surveyed one of the newest arrivals to the Holly Ardath Gallery. The painting they were gazing at was six feet by eleven feet, a canvas of smeared blue and orange paint that from certain angles resembled a fire on an ocean liner, and that from other angles simply resembled an attempt on the part of the painter to create seventy-five thousand dollars' worth of artistic chaos.

"May I get you something to drink?" Patrizia inquired in Italian. The woman glanced back at her, replying that no, she was fine, thank you. Remembering the early days of her art-gallery training, Patrizia took this as a clear sign that the couple should be left alone while they made their decision.

Holly had welcomed Patrizia back to the gallery, giving

a shout of delight when she first came through the doors on a cool, bright Manhattan morning in late September. Unfortunately, despite Holly's assurance that there would always be a job open for Patrizia, the Holly Ardath Gallery was fully staffed. "I wish you'd given me some warning," she said, adding, "Just last month, I had to hire two extra people. The economy here is going through the roof."

Holly must have noted Patrizia's distressed expression, because a moment later she pulled her aside with a proposition: she could hire Patrizia to work at the gallery, but it would have to be part-time, which meant that Patrizia could receive commissions, but she wouldn't be eligible for benefits.

Patrizia left her meeting with Holly worried whether or not she would be able to afford to live in New York City anymore. Manhattan seemed dirtier than she remembered—noisier and more crowded. After Rome, the city had hit her in the face like the blast of a furnace. It wasn't that Patrizia hadn't been reminded of the United States time and again while in Italy. In fact, she couldn't count the number of times she'd been browsing in an Italian store or supermarket while rock anthems sung in English blared from the store speakers. It was that she had simply forgotten how loud and insistent American culture was.

She couldn't stop thinking about Porto Ercole—the silence of the water and the curving hills, the narrow roads and the gently rocking boats roped to the old docks—or about Rome: the churches, the bells, the pigeons, the past and the present effortlessly tied together. Worse, during the month and a half that Patrizia had been in Italy, the price of a New York City apartment seemed to have skyrocketed. Moreover, Lucy, her old roommate, was no longer living in the city. She'd gotten a small role in a television pilot and moved to Los Angeles to pursue her acting career, and when Patrizia had inquired if there were any apartments available in her old building, she discovered to her shock that there was a waiting list.

Instead, she ended up signing a lease on a narrow, L-shaped, one-room apartment in lower Manhattan, halfway between Little Italy and Chinatown, which she shared with a thirty-five-year-old television publicist, who fortunately was rarely at home. For the first few weeks Patrizia found herself gazing miserably out the windows at the rows of hanging laundry, the D and Q trains rumbling over the Manhattan Bridge into Brooklyn. To say the least, living in Little Italy wasn't quite the same as living in Italy. But over time, to her surprise, she found herself feeling more and more settled in New York. She bought plants, and bookcases, and posters for her walls. She made curtains from fabric she'd found in the basement of her mother's house, and she treated herself to an espresso maker from Zabar's.

For the first time in her life, Patrizia realized, she felt at home. During her first few weeks back she discovered to her surprise that she'd adopted an Italian way of thinking about, and even preparing, food. She no longer shopped in supermarkets, or bought food in bulk, but instead simply picked up what she was planning on eating that day at the local green market in Union Square, whether it was tomatoes, basil, peppers, broccoli, or fresh fish. And since Holly needed her to work at the gallery only two or three afternoons a week, Patrizia found that she could devote most of her time to painting.

She wasn't altogether certain how her painting had changed, but it had, and she knew this had something to do with her father. Patrizia knew this much: for the first time in her life someone who mattered to her (for better or for worse) had encouraged her painting. Someone had followed her every step of the way, sometimes with a whip, sometimes with a gentle prod, always goading her on, and ultimately helping her to let go of something crucial inside her that had been blocked for twenty-two years.

It wasn't just that Patrizia found herself painting more fluidly, it was that she *wanted* to paint. All the time. Every single waking moment. She thought about painting constantly—at the gallery, while she was out jogging in the park, while she made fresh espresso in the morning. At times she couldn't wait to leave the gallery and get home and start painting again, since nothing seemed to make her happier than to be alone in her apartment, working endlessly on a single canvas. Over the past few weeks she had produced nearly half a dozen paintings.

Still, she missed Andrea desperately.

Since her return from Rome, Patrizia had puzzled over her own behavior many times. Yet she was positive she had done the right thing by not calling Andrea back, and by leaving. What had he been so eager to tell her anyway—that their relationship was going nowhere, and that he didn't want to see her anymore? No doubt it was some variation of that. While she took some responsibility for distancing herself from him over the past couple of months, she wasn't the only one, was she? The similarities, after all, between Andrea and her father were striking. Both of them handsome, athletic, charming Italian men. Both of them smart, witty, well-spoken, able to converse about a wide range of subjects. Both of them emotionally intense, unable to disguise their feelings. Both of them inordinately proud of their native city, Rome, and their native country. Both of them lovers of food and good cooking. Both of them ardent pursuers of American women.

The way Patrizia had felt around Andrea frightened her: out of control, off balance, passionate. Scared. That was it, Andrea had scared her. Still, she found it difficult to get him out of her mind—and forgetting about him was impossible. His face appeared to her while she slept, as she was painting, as she daydreamed at the gallery, waiting for customers to make up their minds. Patrizia would never get over him, she was certain of that. At the same time she counted herself lucky to have escaped from Andrea, and from Rome, when she had. If Lizzie had taught her anything it was this: Protect yourself. Don't leave yourself vulnerable to any man.

It was much easier for her to convince herself that she had spent her time in Italy missing Eric.

Patrizia had called Eric soon after her return, half expecting that in her absence he had gotten involved with another woman, and in some ways, hoping that he had. At first his voice on the phone was clipped and at times sarcastic. "Thanks a lot for staying in touch with me while you were in Italy," he said at one point, but when Patrizia told him what had happened with Masi and her painting—she left out all the parts that had to do with Andrea—he seemed to soften. "I think you were right after all, Eric," she concluded.

"What was I right about?"

"About me seeing my father."

Eric was silent for a long time. Then he said, "Hey, listen, Patrizia, do you want to have dinner tonight? I have a bunch of papers to correct, but I'd much rather get together with you."

They met for dinner at a small, nearly empty Chinese restaurant in Chelsea, and when Eric saw her, he didn't try to hug her or kiss her. He simply stood there, gazing at her. It was Patrizia who came forward and hugged him. "I missed you so much, Eric," she said after a moment, aware of a sudden hollowness in her stomach.

"I've missed you, too," Eric said. He looked better than she had ever seen him, tanned and handsome.

"How's Katie?" she asked a moment later.

"She's great. She wanted me to say hi to you."

When the food arrived, Patrizia gazed up at Eric. "I've

been thinking about you a lot, and I just wanted to apologize."

"Apologize for what?"

"For not being present for you when you needed me to be." Patrizia was silent.

"So tell me the whole thing: you actually met the guy?"

For the next two hours Patrizia told Eric the whole story. About going to Rome, and finding the Masimilliano Caracci Gallery closed, meeting Becky, then taking the cab ride to Porto Ercole (here, she left out Andrea again), pretending to be Anna Dineen, the painting she had completed, her father's enthusiasm for her work—as well as their final confrontation. Eric listened in silence. "God, Patrizia," he said when she paused for breath. "I wrote you tons of letters—"

"I never got any letters."

"Of course you didn't! I didn't have your address! Why the hell didn't you get in touch with me?"

"I tried!"

"*Once* you tried!"

"It was too expensive. And I"—Patrizia paused—"I didn't really know where I was going to be exactly most of the time." She paused again. "I'm"—she couldn't think of the word—"ready, I guess."

"Ready for what? What are you ready for."

"Ready. To see you. To have a relationship with you." The words came out mechanically, but Eric was nodding his head intently, pleased.

Somewhat reluctantly, she began seeing him again, spending most of her free time over at his apartment on the Upper East Side, and the rest of her time either at work, or alone in her apartment, painting. Katie came to visit, and during those weekends Patrizia spent a lot of time with her, taking her for outings in Central Park and to the Chelsea Piers to go rock climbing, but mostly to museums, where she introduced Katie to Monet and Renoir.

Eric. Katie. Painting. A small apartment in Little Italy. Time and again Patrizia tried to put her finger on what it was that frustrated her about her life, but with little success. Was this simply the aftereffect of meeting Masi for the first time, and finding that ultimately her father was no different from the shadowy figure she'd imagined him to be all her life? Was it simply that having met her father, she now felt a melancholy sense of completion—that in some senses, there was no one, no one thing, to dream about anymore? Was it that she had gone through a transformation in Italy, and upon her return, she'd found that Eric was still living his life as he always had—that he still ate two fried eggs over easy every morning, that he still changed into his pajamas by nine o'clock every night before settling down in front of the TV with a stack of student essays and a bowl of butter-pecan ice cream?

No, it wasn't remotely fair to Eric, but Patrizia could not stop thinking about Andrea, even when she found herself on an airplane flying home to Wisconsin to sign the purchase and sale agreement for her mother's house, which had been bought by a young couple with three children. She even thought about Andrea when she was making love with Eric, and afterward, she hated herself for this silent betrayal.

Patrizia had taken the small amount of money she received from the sale of Lizzie's house and put it in the bank, determined that she would never use it except in case of an emergency. But increasingly over the next several months she found herself eyeing the money, even though business at the gallery continued to thrive. Eventually, she had to start looking around for a full-time job, interviewing at several other SoHo galleries, but finding the same answer at every single one: "Come back in the spring, we might be hiring then." Patrizia would return home to her apartment, exhausted, worried about how she would be able to remain living in New York, though when she'd told this to Eric, his face had fallen.

"Why don't we get married?" he asked her one afternoon. They were sitting on stools in his kitchen, waiting for a large order of Japanese food to be delivered.

"Cool," Patrizia said, convinced Eric was joking. "Shall we do it tonight or tomorrow? Actually, wait, tomorrow I can't, I have to work."

"Anytime you want," Eric said slightly sadly, and a moment later Patrizia realized that if he wasn't entirely serious himself, he'd been testing her to find out what her reaction would be. Feeling guilty at having been so flippant, she took a seat next to him, and squeezed his hand.

"I'd be a terrible wife," she told him gently. "I'd always have paint all over me, and I'd reek of turpentine."

They hadn't discussed the possibility of marriage since. And it was on a cold, overcast Saturday afternoon in January when Patrizia finally made the decision to leave New York and move back home to the Midwest. That night, the city was digging out from a blizzard that had temporarily shut down businesses, caused bus service to be canceled, and stranded motorists on highways. She had spent a few hours at Holly's gallery that morning, but by noontime, when the snow began falling in earnest, Holly ordered everybody, including the four customers who were looking at paintings, to go home. "Everybody out," she said. "I'm going home myself to build a snowman."

At home, Patrizia discovered that unknown to her, the pipes in her apartment had frozen and that there was no heat coming out of the radiators. Panicked, she tried to reach her landlord without success, and on her fourth attempt to call a plumber, the receptionist on the other end of the line informed her that plumbing rates doubled on the weekends. "It comes out to four hundred dollars," she said, and incredulous, Patrizia had no choice but to agree.

Later that afternoon, after the plumber had come and gone, Patrizia sat down on her bed and attempted to calculate her living expenses at least until summer came. She had little sense of how much money she might earn in commissions from Holly's gallery, and the landlord would doubtlessly reimburse her for the cost of the plumber's visit, but the truth was staring her in the face: unless she began raiding the proceeds from the sale of her mother's house, her money would dry up in April. Panicked and disconsolate, she put on her jacket and took a long walk in the snow. As she passed by Grand Street, the sound of sirens ripped through the streets, followed, several minutes later, by the shriek of a passing ambulance.

New York City seemed suddenly unlivable, unbearable to Patrizia. Where was the beauty in this kind of a life, worried about money all the time, surrounded by ugly buildings and harried people? What in the world was keeping her here?

The next day, she informed her roommate that she would be moving back to the Midwest at the end of the month. She would rent a room in her old hometown, maybe an apartment atop someone's garage, with a separate stairwell. Argyle, Wisconsin, was full of empty spaces. There she could live cheaply, find a part-time job, and paint. In time she might move to Milwaukee, possibly even Chicago. The lake. The Loop. The Art Institute. She could find an apartment, a roommate, maybe even rent a light-filled studio. Yet despite these fantasies, the notion of picking up her belongings and starting afresh in a new place, however familiar, still felt deflating.

The hardest part about leaving New York was breaking the news to Eric, though Patrizia was almost certain that he'd be relieved. Ever since he had brought up the idea of getting married, and she had made a joke out of it, he had been acting noticeably cool around her. Worse, she hadn't really minded. But wasn't this the best way to break up with him? Simply to leave New York? She would be meeting him for dinner on the Upper West Side on Friday night, and she planned to tell him then.

For the next few days Patrizia reluctantly began making moving arrangements: reserving a U-Haul to transport her belongings back to the Midwest in three weeks' time, and alerting real-estate agents in her hometown to be on the lookout for a reasonably priced one-bedroom apartment. Holly took the news badly. "You can't leave New York, Patrizia!" she exclaimed. "You *belong* here. Plus, I thought you told me you were really starting to feel settled here!"

"I was," Patrizia said. "It's just, I feel like I belong back at home, that's all."

The afternoon after she'd informed Holly of her plans Patrizia trudged home through the icy New York streets, climbed the three flights of stairs, and let herself into her apartment. As usual, the first thing she did was water her plants and scan her mail. There was nothing that day, she would remember later, just some bills, a couple of magazines that her roommate subscribed to (*Us, Entertainment Weekly*), as well as a threatening notice from Con Edison. Afterward, she switched on various lights, trying to create a fortress against the gray, snowy winter afternoon. She had just prepared herself a cup of green tea and was bringing it into the living room, when she heard the knock at the front door.

Assuming it was Sally, her roommate, who made a

habit of forgetting her key and locking herself out, Patrizia rose slowly. "Hello," she called out. She peered through the peephole, and saw the top of someone's head, as well as a slight growth of beard. Her heart began to pound, and a second later she threw open the door.

Andrea was standing there, attired in a scarf and a dark blue parka, grinning down at Patrizia, at his feet two bags, one of them a large black duffel, the other a white canvas carry-on with thick red straps. "Do you remember me?" he said at last.

Despite herself, Patrizia rushed forward and hugged him as hard as she could, burying her face against the soft down of his coat. "Don't cry," Andrea was saying. "My God, Patrizia, I thought you might be glad to see me, not sad."

"I'm not sad," she managed to blurt out. "I'm *so* happy." She took a step backward, taking a long look at him. "You look great," she blurted out. "But—"

"Let me guess. You are going to ask me, What I am doing here in New York City, right?"

"Right," Patrizia replied uncertainly, aware that her heart was still pounding in her chest. A moment later she was hugging Andrea again, her lips meeting his.

She ushered him into the apartment. "Sit down. Have you just come from the airport or something? How in the world did you know where I lived anyway?"

"Your father told me, I think."

Patrizia stopped short. "My father?" she repeated slowly.

"Yes. Signore Caracci. He's your father."

It wasn't a question, it was a statement. "Right," she said at last. Then, in a rush: "Look, Andrea, I'm sorry I didn't tell you, but I couldn't."

Andrea was looking at her strangely. "Will you sit down, please?"

"How did he know where I live?"

"He called your mother's friend. Sarah—"

"Sarah?" Patrizia repeated, incredulous.

"Yes, your godmother. She wouldn't speak to Signore Caracci at first, but finally, when he explained the situation, they talked. She told him where you worked, where you were living. She would not give him your phone number, just your address."

Sarah. Patrizia wouldn't have thought it possible. She had spoken several times with her godmother over the past several weeks, but not once had she mentioned her trip to Italy, or her father. Just recently, she'd asked Sarah if she would keep her ears open for any vacant apartments in Milwaukee or Chicago.

"Will you sit down, please?" Andrea repeated.

Noticing the serious expression on his face, she did as he said. A moment later Andrea handed her the canvas bag. "Actually, Patrizia," he said in a soft voice, "I don't have good news for you."

"What is it?" she asked, suddenly anxious.

Andrea gestured at the white canvas carry-on bag. A large cardboard tube was sticking out from the top, and for no good reason, Patrizia's heart sank. What had Masi sent her? Had she left something behind in Rome by accident?

There were, it seemed, two distinct parts of the package. The first was a white envelope bound around a smaller envelope, this one with an official-looking letterhead, and Patrizia knew from her limited knowledge of Italian that *avvocato* meant lawyer. The letter, when she slowly opened it, was in English, obviously for her sake.

Dear Ms. Orman:

It is my regret to inform you that your father Masimilliano Caracci, passed away from lung cancer last month at the age of forty-five. According to the terms of his last will and testament, it was Mr. Caracci's intention that you have the accompanying painting. If you have any other questions, please do not hesitate to contact us.

Sincerely,
Roberto Pisanelli, avvocato

Tears sprang to Patrizia's eyes, tears mixed with disbelief. It had to be a mistake: Masi, dead of cancer? Hurriedly, she tore open the other letter and pulled out a typewritten note. Glancing down at the signature, she saw that it was from her father. She handed it to Andrea. "I can't read this, it's in Italian."

"But it's very personal, I think."

"Andrea, I want to know what it says."

Andrea took the letter from her. "I will do my best." He cleared his throat, and haltingly translated:

Dear Patrizia:

By the time you receive this letter, I will be gone. Unfortunately, a lifetime of bad habits has caught up with me. Do you remember in Porto Ercole how many times I would go into Rome? I told you that these visits were for business, but they were not. I was seeing my doctor, who a year ago found what looked like a small storm on my left lung. It is worth saying to you again: please do not smoke. This makes me sad for me, of course, but it makes me more sad for you, because even though you left me so angry, when people die, it affects others, and even though you do not wish to see me, or speak with me, it was probably, I am guessing, a helpful thing maybe to know that somewhere in the world there was a father who loved you very much.

I write this letter to you to explain the sort of person that I am, and that I fear I have always been. I have always found it difficult to settle down with a single person. I feel as if all my freedoms will be taken away if I do this. It is a struggle for me, my love of a woman versus my love of solitude. Usually, in the end, my love of the habit of solitude wins this struggle. I loved your mother, Lizzie, very much, and I hurt her very much.

For a man, accomplishment usually becomes the paramount thing in his life, and he often will put love and family second. This is wrong, but it is often what men are born with.

Twenty-two years ago it was more important for me to succeed in what I did than it was to have a family. I had a demanding father, and I wanted him to love me, and to approve of me. He was not around much, and so I did not learn from him what it means to be a father. You asked me once, what does it mean to be a father to a daughter? I think in answer to your question that to be a father is a lot like being a mother: it is to nurture, and to hold, and to support, and to protect, and to give confidence to your children so that they can grow up to be in all ways better than you are.

I bought this painting for you the moment I began making a good living, almost fifteen years ago. It reminded me of the girl, and the artist, I thought you would someday become. Look at how the artist renders this beautiful child: she is utterly enraptured as she reads the book she is holding. You know she will succeed in the world, learn from others' mistakes—including her parents', and especially her father's—and that she will become who she wants to be.

In France, the painting is called Le Livre d'Images. *In English, I believe it is known simply as* The Picture Book. *Auguste Renoir painted it in*

1898, and while I do not generally love Renoirs—I must admit I find him a little bit sappy—I love this one very much. I send it in care of your friend Andrea, who I have found out loves my daughter very, very much. I know that you probably do not need my blessing to be with any man, that my blessing is irrelevant to what you do, but if it means anything at all to you, he is a good man, a man I would be happy to see by your side for the rest of your life.

Do what you want with the painting. Several months ago a similar painting by Renoir sold at Christie's auction house in New York for many, many millions of dollars, U.S. I hope that owning this will free you from any financial constraints that you may have suffered in your life. I have also transferred the deed to I Perazzi in Porto Ercole to your name. Again, you may do with the property as you like (though I must admit to a secret wish that you keep it in our family). I do not think I shall forget easily the sight of a young girl standing out on the lawn with her easel, finally trusting herself to paint what her eye was able to see at last so clearly. I hope that you will come back to I Perazzi often, to paint, or to do whatever you wish. It belongs to you.

We did not leave each other well. We were both so angry and disappointed at each other. I am sorry. I am sorry that I cannot change. But life, as you will find out, is not like the fairy tales that we so wrongly grow up with as our examples of how people behave. People have good qualities, and less good qualities. Life is never black and white, but instead, various shades of gray. The older you get, the more the colors of gray increase. By then you are an old man—and a child somewhere is being instructed that life is painted in black and white. And so the wheels keep turning.

You have all my love, forever, Patrizia. I am very, very proud of you.

Your loving father

Patrizia could not stop crying, though she did not know what she was crying for exactly. It was not for the painting—at that moment she did not even dare open the thick cardboard tube—but for the letter her father had written her, for the lifetime of anger and confusion it summed up, and that it was now attempting to close. She could not believe that Masi, her father, was gone. And she could not believe that for fifteen years he had been saving a painting for her. A painting by Lizzie's favorite artist, and most important, a painting that had reminded him of the little girl he'd never met.

"You came back to me," Patrizia heard herself saying to Andrea.

Despite the solemnity of the moment, Andrea grinned at her. "Of course I came back to you, Patrizia. I told you, I love you."

When Patrizia hadn't returned his phone calls, he explained, he had gone straight to Masi's gallery, "in the hope that Signore Caracci might know where I could find you." Andrea blushed at the memory of this. "Anyhow, your father told me everything. Everything about your mother, everything about the past. He told me about his health. He'd known he was dying for a long time, since the beginning of the summer. I think it was good for him to have you there. It gave him a chance again to be a father to a girl he'd never known." Andrea was silent. "It was your father who told me I must go find you. He said, 'You cannot let this happen in another generation. It is too much of a waste of love. Do not end up a fool, all by yourself, the way I am—' "

"He wasn't a fool," Patrizia broke in angrily.

"No," Andrea said softly. "He wasn't a fool at all."

Patrizia stared at Andrea, and a moment later she gingerly removed part of the painting from the tube, allowing the majesty of the Renoir to fill her tiny apartment.

"Oh my God," was Andrea's awed response, and Patrizia could not find anything at all to add. At last she said, "I will never sell this painting." It was the truth. She would sooner part with her blood or a part of her body than sell the Renoir. A moment later she added, very softly, "My father gave it to me."